THE HIDDEN CHORUS

THE HIDDEN CHORUS

NY WRITERS COALITION PRESS
BROOKLYN ~ 2008

Copyright © 2008 NY Writers Coalition Inc.

ALL RIGHTS RESERVED. Upon publication, copyright to individual works returns to the authors.

Published by NY Writers Coalition Press, a division of NY Writers Coalition Inc., Brooklyn, New York. For orders and information please contact

NY Writers Coalition Inc.
80 Hanson Place #603
Brooklyn, NY 11217
(718) 398-2883
info@nywriterscoalition.org
www.nywriterscoalition.org

ISBN-13: 9780978779429
ISBN: 0978779428
Printed and bound in the Canada
Library of Congress Control Number: 2008932025

Book & cover design: Christian Peet, Tarpaulin Sky Design (www.tarpaulinsky.com)
Title font: Slurry
Text font: Adobe Garamond Pro

CONTENTS

Preface: About New York Writers Coalition   i

Introduction   vii

MAMA PICKS OUT MY CLOTHES

Mama Picks Out My Clothes   3
EVGENIA BENETATOS, AGE 9

My Babies   4
CANDACE SHEPHARD

My Dad   5
BASMA AZZAMOK, AGE 7

‼ That So Called Sister ‼   6
JOLEE COHEN, AGE 10

Italian Double Take   7
MARY P. BLAS

I'm Sorry   9
EVGENIA BENETATOS, AGE 9

Driving Force   10
ADRIANA RICCI

A Woman   11
MALIK GARNETT, AGE 12

Advice   12
FATIMA HILL

Margaret and the Black and Tans   13
EILEEN D. KELLY

Dad   18
BRIAN LEONG, AGE 7

The Vessel Fillers   19
MARIETTA MASON

When   22
MICHELLE BROADY

Ferris Wheel   23
DWIGHT SMITH

Tony   24
KIM STORMS

Mom   25
VIRDAH ZAMAN, AGE 14

Aniya Imani   26
LISA WASHINGTON

A Faraway Gift   27
MYRA BAUM

I SHALL DOTE MYSELF

I Shall Dote Myself   31
ALMEDIA S. KNIGHT

Recipe for Shunn   33
SHUNN THEINGI, AGE 11

Untitled (looking at photographs of faces)   34
QIIYANA SIMPKINS, AGE 17

My Name   35
BRIAN LEONG, AGE 7

I Think Not   36
JACQUELINE MURRAY

Because   37
MIKHAL MORRIS, AGE 11

The History In Me   38
NAJAYA ROYAL, AGE 10

Dear Nose   39
JUSTINA JORDAN

I Am a Car   40
MARIE ANICET, AGE 16

I Used To   41
BRIDIN MCCANN, AGE 6

Look Up   42
DONNA M. DICKERSON

The Right Fit   43
JACQUELINE MURRAY

Where I Am From   44
SHAQUANNA COLE

I Am   45
SOMAYAH ALJAHMI, AGE 12

IS THIS ALL REAL?

Looking Out of the Window   49
LORRAINE BEYER THEORDOR

I Am From the Ghetto   50
MALIK GARNETT, AGE 12

Out My Window   51
BASMA AZZAMOK, AGE 7

Easter   52
CARLOS GARCIA

Home at Last   53
PAUL FRANCOIS, AGE 11

Blinding   54
JOLEE COHEN, AGE 10

Hot Day in Brooklyn   55
MYRA BAUM

My Block   57
CARLOS GARCIA

Il Monde in the Profane   58
PAT JACKSON

What's Next?   60
MATTIE LIVINGSTONE

Blue Sky   61
JUSTINA JORDAN

Haiku for Spring   62
CAROLE BEAUBIEN GREGORY

Magical Room   63
NANCY BECK

Ghetto   64
NAJAYA ROYAL, AGE 10

Sounds   65
VERONIKA ANTONIADIS, AGE 13

Untitled   66
JENNY LYNN ADAMES

MARY KATHRYN'S BELIEFS

Mary Kathryn's Beliefs   69
MARY KATE TRAMONTANO, AGE 6

What Money Can't Buy   70
SHIRLEY N. BLAND

January's End   71
MICHAEL COOK

Thanks   72
LINDA THOMAS

I Thought I Saw God   73
FRANCES BUSCHKE

LUIGI ALMOST BROKE MY CELL PHONE

Luigi Almost Broke My Cell Phone   77
MARILYN SOLARES, AGE 12

Broken Things Want   78
BARRY BLITSTEIN

Nine Ways of Looking at Him   79
GENESIS NIARA LEE

First Love   81
ALLEN HOAGE

She Was My Project   82
VAN EVERKOOL

BC Charm   84
PRECIOUS WILSON

Untitled   85
RAQUEL HILL

Ode to Elton   86
DYANE L. MILLER

Spring Time Is My Time   87
RUBY ELLERBE SCOTT

TRYING TO GET EVEN

Trying To Get Even   91
BOB ROSEN

Bored of Education   96
GEORGE LANTAY

When I Fell   97
MARILYN SOLARES, AGE 12

You Think You're Hiding   98
BARRY BLITSTEIN

If Not Now   99
ARK STONE

Race   101
SHIRLEY N. BLAND

Trustworthiness   102
ZOE EIFFEL

Untitled   103
GERRY BOGACZ

Love Lost   104
ARK STONE

No More   106
KIM STORMS

Prejudice   107
LINDA THOMAS

One Ghost To Another   108
THERESA KEIS

Rude Awakening   109
SUZANNE LAPKA

Untitled   110
RAQUEL HILL

Vampire and Werewolf   111
PRECIOUS WILSON

Diamond   113
CARMEN COCEPTION

Untitled   114
JENNY LYNN ADAMES

I Am From   115
NAJAYA ROYAL, AGE 10

The Tightrope   116
MURIEL GRAY

To My Favorite Lucy						117
RAQUEL HILL

HERE IS WHERE I ESCAPE

Here is where I escape...					121
BY SHAQUANNA COLE

I Pray You, Our Artist						122
DEV ROGERS

Strange Fruit							123
LORRAINE BEYER THEORDOR

Paradox								124
ZOE EIFFEL

Sonnet								125
BOB ROSEN

Where Does Creativity Come From?			126
THERESA KEIS

Magician							127
PAT JACKSON

WHEN IT ALL BECOMES TRUE

When It All Becomes True					131
LISA FENGER

Imagine								136
VERONIKA ANTONIADIS, AGE 13

Reverie of My Haiti						137
CAROLE DEEB

The Creek							139
CLAUDE H. OLIVER II

Destination: Promised Land					141
SUZANNE LAPKA

Untitled   143
GERRY BOGACZ

I Thought You Should Know   144
ANNE SAMACHSON

THERE IS A MAN I KNOW WHO LIKES TO PUT GLITTER ON HIS CLOTHES

Submarine   157
JUSTINA JORDAN

Magic's Address   158
JEDIAEL S. FRASER, AGE 8

If I Were A Kite   159
CAITLYN KLENNER, AGE 7

Seven Wonders   160
PEGGY LIEGEL

Rita Dove   161
PAUL FRANCOIS, AGE 11

Cloud Pink Cake   162
LEEN SHUMMAN, AGE 8

The Promise   163
ALLAN YASHIN

Funny Day   171
SHUNN THEINGI, AGE 11

I Never   174
DONALD WILLIAMS

Sucked In   175
JOSEPH FRANCOIS, AGE 9

Paper Bag   176
CAITLYN KLENNER, AGE 7

The Fox in the Bush JEDIAEL S. FRASER, AGE 8	177
The Man Is Jungle Dog JUDE	178
An Ode to Snow OSOSE EBESUNUN, AGE 9	180
Goldfish MARIE LIVINGSTON	181
The Big Blue Box VICTOR SANCHEZ, AGE 10	182
The Adventure VINCENT SANCHEZ, AGE 12	183
My Third Eye HAYAT DHOBHANY, AGE 9	184
Telephone Poem QIIYANA SIMPKINS, AGE 17	185
Waiting SYD LAZARUS	186
Green ISAIAH SANCHEZ, AGE 9	187
My Ode To Fall (Oh Apple Pie) TANZANIA COLEMAN, AGE 9	188
Butterflies are Cool MYINT MYAT THINN KYI, AGE 8	189
Autobiography of the Color Red KARLA CONFORD	190
Fortune Cookie ANDREW LEONG, AGE 8	192
Her Name Was Lucky ALLEN RAYMON	193

My Only Friends   194
ISAIAH SANCHEZ, AGE 9

The Nose Never Lies   195
BY JOSEPH FRANCOIS, AGE 9

My Morning Ride   196
ALLEN HOAGE

Wheels on the Bus   197
MYINT MYAT THINN KYI, AGE 8

The Moon   198
ANDREW LEONG, AGE 8

White Nightgowns   199
MURIEL GRAY

Earring   200
MIKHAL MORRIS, AGE 11

The Year I Turned 10   201
BY JOSEPH FRANCOIS, AGE 9

Mirror, Mirror on the Wall   202
SYD LAZARUS

PREFACE

About New York Writers Coalition (NYWC)

NYWC, a 501(c)3 not-for-profit organization creates opportunities for formerly voiceless members of society to be heard through the art of writing. We provide free, unique and powerful creative writing workshops throughout New York City for people from groups that have been historically deprived of voice in our society, including at-risk youth, adult residents of supportive housing, the formerly incarcerated, seniors and others.

NYWC is one of the largest community-based writing organizations in the country. In the past year, we conducted over one thousand workshop sessions at approximately 45 locations, creating ongoing writing communities throughout the city. We've published numerous anthologies of writing by our workshop members as well as Plum Biscuit, an online literary magazine edited by our workshop members. NYWC also operates the Writing Aloud reading series, a monthly event featuring members of our workshops reading alongside established authors; Write Makes Might, an annual marathon reading by our workshop members; and is a partner in the annual Fort Greene Park Summer Literary Festival, a series of writing workshops for young people culminating in a reading by the young writers with literary icons such as Amiri Baraka, Jhumpa Lahiri, Sonia Sanchez and Sapphire. Workshop participants have had poems, stories and plays published and performed. Others have read their writing on NPR's All Things Considered, WNYC's Brian Lehrer Show and WBAI's Global Movements, Urban Struggles.

As a small, grassroots organization, NYWC relies on the generous support of those dedicated to getting the voices heard of those who have been silenced. Thanks go to our foundation, government and corporate supporters, including Time Warner's Youth Media and Arts Fund, the Hot Topic Foundation, the Independence Community Foundation, the Kalliopeia Foundation, the Pinkerton Foundation, the Union Square Arts Awards, Valentine Perry Snyder Fund, the NYC Department of Cultural Affairs, the NY State Council For The Arts, NY State Senator Velmanette Montgomery, and others for their generous support.

We also rely heavily on the support of many individuals. Our workshop leaders have volunteered thousands of hours because they believe in giving back to their communities. Many others have made financial contributions and attended our events. Thanks go to NYWC Program Director Deborah Clearman for doing all three of these things (volunteering, making donations and attending everything!). In addition, our Board of Directors, Stacy Abramson, Kara Gilmour, Frank Haberle, and Executive Director Aaron Zimmerman, have stewarded us through the joyous struggle to keep our vital work going. To find out how you can support us by becoming a member or participating in our annual Write-A-Thon, please visit www.nywriterscoalition.org.

This anthology contains some of the writing created by our workshop members from September 2005 through May 2007. Most of the writing in this book was created during our workshops, gathered in a room with other writers. Participants from NYWC's workshops were invited to submit work of their own choosing, and writing from everyone that submitted is included. Writers made all editorial decisions about their own work. The editorial committee, made up of NYWC staff and volunteers, read all submitted work and when appropriate, selected writing from a range of pieces by a given writer. We take great pride in our efforts to be inclusive, and to present the writers' work in their true, beautiful voices. Many thanks to Mary Ellen Sanger, proofreader extraordinaire, and to Christian Peet, design genius.

NYWC Workshop Sites and Leaders

Writers included in this anthology participated in workshops at one of the below listed locations.

Arab-American Family Support Center: A workshop for children of recent Arab immigrants in Downtown Brooklyn. Workshop leaders: Erin Hopkins, Nancy Weber.

Atlantic Terminal Senior Center: A day center for seniors in public housing in Brooklyn. Workshop leader: Deborah Clearman.

Audubon Hall: Supportive housing in Washington Heights. Workshop leader: Beau Karch.

Blossom Program For Girls: A program for teenage girls at high risk of gang involvement in Bedford-Stuyvesant, Brooklyn, operated by Youth Empowerment Mission Inc. Workshop Leader: Sophie McManus.

Brooklyn Public Library, New Lots Branch: A program for teens and kids living in East New York. Workshop leader: Angeli Rasbury.

Brooklyn Public Library, Eastern Parkway Branch: A program for Crown Heights teens and kids. Workshop leader: Angeli Rasbury.

Children's Aid Society: A youth development program for teens returning from incarceration in E. Harlem. Workshop leader: Kesha Young.

Fort Greene Park Summer Literary Festival: Two summer-long, outdoor writing workshops for young people in Fort Greene, Brooklyn. Workshop Leaders: Various NYWC volunteers.

Fort Greene Seniors: A workshop for seniors in Fort Greene, Brooklyn. Workshop Leader: Madeline George.

Fourteenth Street Y Educational Center for Retired Adults: A program of classes for older adults, operated by The Educational Alliance. Workshop Leader: Deborah Clearman.

Imani House: An after school program for elementary school children, providing support and assistance to immigrant and economically disadvantaged residents of the community, at P.S. 282 in Park Slope, Brooklyn. Workshop Leader: Erin Hopkins.

Jan Hus Church Homeless Outreach and Advocacy Program: Direct services for homeless people on the Upper West Side. Workshop Leader: Andrea Chalupa.

Judson Hall Residence For Women: Women's residence in downtown Brooklyn operated by the YWCA of Brooklyn. Workshop Leader: Sheryl Gordon.

NY Public Library Aguilar Language Learning Center: Program of classes in Adult Basic Education and ESOL in East Harlem. Workshop Leader: Amie Hartman.

Prime Time: A program for people over 50 living in the rapidly gentrifying area of Clinton Hill, Brooklyn, operated by Emmanuel Baptist Church. Workshop Leader: Debra Kirschner.

Queens Public Library, Broadway Branch: Workshop for kids in the diverse community of Long Island City. Workshop Leaders: Barbara Cassidy, Mary Smith.

Ridge Girls: A program for teen girls in Brooklyn Public Library, Bay Ridge Branch. Workshop Leader: Barbara Cassidy.

SAGE: Community center for GLBT elders. Workshop Leader: Rachel Kahn.

Stay N Out / Serendipity: Residence in Bedford-Stuyvesant, Brooklyn, for formerly incarcerated women seeking substance abuse treatment, operated by NY Therapeutic Communities. Workshop Leader: Suzanne Guillette.

Sylvia's Place: An emergency night shelter for homeless LGBT teens at the Metropolitan Community Church in Manhattan. Workshop Leader: Tamiko Beyer.

The Creative Center: Arts center for people living with cancer in Manhattan. Workshop Leader: Clarissa Cummings.

World Trade Center Survivors Network: A support and advocacy group for survivors of the attacks on the World Trade Center. Workshop Leader: Melanie O'Harra.

INTRODUCTION

The Hidden Chorus

It's hard to believe that NY Writers Coalition (NYWC) started out of Executive Director Aaron Zimmerman's home just six short years ago, running only a handful of free creative writing workshops for formerly voiceless members of society. Since then NYWC has grown exponentially, to the point that in the past year we operated over one thousand workshops in 45 different locations for an extremely diverse group of wonderfully talented New Yorkers, from a variety of all-too-often silenced groups, such as at-risk youth and teens, seniors, people with mental illness, those affected by cancer, people with HIV/AIDS, people living in supportive housing, the formerly homeless, domestic abuse survivors, the formerly incarcerated, and survivors of the September 11 attacks on the World Trade Center.

One of the most exciting aspects of putting together this Anthology was seeing this growth reflected—both in sheer number and diversity of voices—in the many pieces we received from workshop members. At NYWC we believe:

That everyone is a writer, regardless of prior writing experience and formal education; Through encouragement and support, people grow as writers and artists;
In the value of the uniqueness of every individual's voice;
Each person's experiences are a source of strength and power as a writer and an artist;
In creating and maintaining a non-judgmental, open and respectful

community where everyone is encouraged to support and listen to each other and to take risks and grow as writers;
Each person, through writing, can shape and influence the lives of others; and
We can achieve social change by providing access and opportunity for all writers, regardless of race, ethnicity, class, age, gender, sexual orientation and physical ability.

The most thrilling part of editing this book was to read the proof of our convictions on the page, to hear just how loudly, strongly, and beautifully the voices that comprise this Anthology sing. In the pages to follow you will find the story of a young Irish woman's emigration to America in the 1920s, a six year-old girl's description of her belief system, a 12 year-old boy's depiction of the ghetto, a woman's memories of her native Haiti, and many, many other absorbing, enchanting, and vibrant stories and poems, from writers of all ages, from every corner of New York City, all from groups and communities not heard from often enough. Each piece on its own is a gem; all of them gathered together in this Anthology is a pulsing, moving, inclusive portrait of New York in the year 2008.

We hope you will enjoy listening to the voices of *The Hidden Chorus* as much as we have.

    Jamila Allidina
    Deborah Clearman
    Raina Wallens
    Nancy Weber

MAMA PICKS OUT MY CLOTHES

MAMA PICKS OUT MY CLOTHES
Evgenia Benetatos, Age 9

Pick Pick Pick
Pick Pink Pink
Pink Pink Pink
Pink Pink Pink
Pink Pink Pink
Pink Pink Pink
Pink Pink Pink
Pink Pink Pink
Pink Pink Pink
Pink Pink Pink
Pink Pink Pink
Pink Pink Pink
Pink Pink Pink
Pink Pink Pink
Pink Pink Pink
Pink Pink Pink
Pink Pink Pink
Pink Pink Pink
Clothing.

MY BABIES
Candace Shephard

Dana Michelle Fuentes
Angela Marie Shephard
These are my babies
The only two I have.
I love them unconditionally.
Angie has a few quirks about her
        -the drugs
        -the blue hair
        -the con game
But I still love her and always will.
No matter what they do,
        Angie and Dana
They are my babies.
They are of my flesh and of my blood.
They are of my DNA which runs
        through their veins.
When their feelings get hurt
I hurt.
When they cry, I cry.
They are of my heart and of my soul.
Maybe, one day, we can go to the beach as a family.
We never did that before.
I would love to have my children together,
        but Angela's ways make it hard to trust her.
But you know what?
I still love her.
Dana Michelle Fuentes
Angela Marie Shephard
Flesh of my flesh and blood of my blood.
My babies.

MY DAD
Basma Azzamok, Age 7

This is my Dad
He works like a taxi man
He looks handsome
He works at night
On Wednesdays he doesn't go to work
He likes to read newspapers
He knows how to ride inline skates
He likes to eat hard chicken
These are the things about my Dad

‼ THAT SO CALLED SISTER ‼
Jolee Cohen, Age 10

She'd whine and whine
and beg and beg
and cry and cry
and he'd say no
and she would say why.
He would say because
and she would say because why
and because she was annoying him
he would let her do
what she wanted to do
and that got on my
nerve. That girl,
that annoying girl,
crying and crying
begging and begging
whining and whining
that so called sister

ITALIAN DOUBLE TAKE
Mary P. Blas

The street is cobbled at its best spots—often it is just dirt and rock. And it is so dry and dusty here. The houses lining this winding street are small one and two story affairs. I can see that there is something going on—women are leaving their houses with pans resting on their hips, arms embracing the pans to prevent the contents from spilling.

A young woman in her late twenties exits one of the houses. She is wearing a dark dress. Wisps of her chestnut-colored hair peek out from the kerchief covering her head. She is lean and muscular and there is something familiar about her. I must get closer.

How strange—she could be me, thirty-five years younger.

I follow her. She joins several other women and they form a small procession as they walk towards the center of town. Now I can see better—they are leaving their pans at a large brick oven. Older women are placing the pans on long pallets and sliding them into the oven. There is much chatter now. It sounds like Italian, but not the Italian I've heard in Fellini movies. It is a dialect I have heard as a child, but cannot understand.

She is finally leaving the clutch of women. Several children have joined her. They are pulling at her skirts. "Mama, Mama!" they shout. And then the Italian I cannot understand. She says –"No! No!" That, I do understand. The oldest boy tells them in English, "Leave Mama alone! She's tired. She's been up all morning baking."

I introduce myself to the boy. His name is Gerardo. I ask

him what the children are saying. He tells me they are begging to have fresh bread for supper that night. I ask why Mama said no. He explains. They can never eat newly baked bread—it would not last. It must become hard—like hardtack—at least a week old before they can eat it drizzled with olive oil, or soaked in coffee if they have had some that morning, or perhaps under soup to stretch a meal.

I ask the boy where he learned English. He proudly tells me that he is an American citizen. He was born in New York. He, his mother, and his six siblings were sent back to Italy to await Papa. Papa will join them as soon as he has made his fortune from his ice business. Then Gerardo tells me that he and his family have been in this remote Southern Italian hill town for two years. When they arrived in 1911, he thought Papa would follow in a few months. But his Papa is having a hard time leaving America. Papa says America is like fly paper—the more you pull away, the more you get stuck!

I ask the boy his mother's name—she looks so familiar. Maria Felice, he informs me. Funny, I tell him. My name is Mary Phyllis—English for Maria Felice. My father Gerry named me after his mother.

I'M SORRY
Evgenia Benetatos, Age 9

I'm sorry that I broke
your house and took your mouse.
I'm sorry that I lit fire on your
house, and I'm sorry that I'm
a liar. I'm sorry that I don't
wipe my shoes. I'm sorry
that I can't speak Greek and
I can't eat cheese. I'm
sorry that I took all
your jam and your
drum. I'm sorry
Grandma.

DRIVING FORCE
Adriana Ricci

My driving force in my life is my son. I adore him completely & totally. It seems to people on the outside looking in that if I loved him so, I wouldn't have done what I did & ultimately hurt him, became separated from him. In my desperation to give him the material life that I thought he needed, I felt that my place wasn't so important. Today, my driving force once again is him, through my faith in God. I'm receiving blessings each and every day, even when I don't think it's possible to receive any more. I have to keep my eye on the prize, which actually could be having my son home with me, but it might not turn out that way. The final prize may very well be just being whole again.

My past has dictated my future for way too long. I can no longer allow that to happen. Because, if I do, it will stunt my growth & I will stay on the pity pot. Then, sooner or later the criminal, addictive thinking will come back into play, but stronger than ever. I've learned to leave the past where it belongs & learn from my mistakes. So I'll know the telltale signs if something should ever start to go wrong. I know that I never want to be the person that I used to be for the obvious reasons! I know that I have lots of potential, lots to offer, & lots of willingness to do the right thing. I'm willing to go through what's needed this time to get to that rainbow.

I'm not leaving until the miracle happens this time. God has done amazing things for me and has given me so much strength and I'm doing all the right things and I have to continue doing them no matter how hard things get. My sins have been forgiven by my Heavenly Father; nobody else needs to forgive me who hasn't forgiven me already.

A WOMAN
Malik Garnett, Age 12

My mother, a strong, powerful, and graceful woman.
The one who gave birth to me.
The one who takes care of me.
The one who feeds me.
The one who clothes me.
The one who sacrifices her time and wants for me.
My mother, the woman I love, hug, and kiss.
The best woman I know in the world.
I will shed blood, sweat, and tears for my strong,
powerful, and graceful mother.

ADVICE
Fatima Hill

She sit her daughter down and
tell her life is full of joy. A
book of your life is what you
write. Laughter enlightens the heart.
Courage strengthens independence.
Anxiousness stresses determination.
Fear strengthens your weakness.
Joy strengthens prosperity. Always
remember the little engine
that can. And you will achieve all goals
and remain happy.

MARGARET AND THE BLACK AND TANS
Eileen D. Kelly

The truckload of British occupation soldiers, the Black and Tans, rushed suddenly and noisily across the border from Protestant Northern Ireland, to the south, into the tiny village of Kiltyclogher in Catholic Leitrim. The warriors jumped down from their vehicle and began looking around menacingly. The few people in the street dashed into their homes or doorways. Some were so terrified they jumped into ditches. The sight of these men dressed in black pants and tan shirts, struck terror in people's hearts. They were known to torture, kill, burn down farmhouses and kidnap, in their pursuit of IRA members and anyone suspected of harboring or associating with them. And, as seems to happen in wars, they often raped and brutalized innocent villagers just because they could.

The year was 1918; WW I was still raging across Europe, and Ireland was busy fighting its rebellion against England. The Easter uprising of 1916 had been suppressed by the British, but the newly formed Irish Republican Army continued its insurgency.

A pretty, green-eyed fourteen year old girl with dark hair, Margaret Sweeney, my mother, was working alone in McGowan's general store. She was sewing her torn felt slipper. Not everyone had shoes or boots, which were generally worn only outdoors in an effort to conserve precious leather. Bare feet or slippers made of fabric were the indoor custom in the poor farming areas of western Ireland.

Margaret saw the rifle-wielding soldiers heading for her shop and in a panic stuck the sewing needle into the slipper, and put it on her foot. With heart pounding she politely asked the men, "May I help you?" Several of them at once demanded, "Cigarettes!" She handed over all the cigarettes she could find in the store. Two of the soldiers gave her a few pence. The rest did not pay anything but left peacefully with their bounty of tobacco. My mother then took off her slipper and saw that the needle had gone into her foot and she couldn't get it out. Throughout her later life she claimed the needle never came out.

Margaret had been taken out of school, which she loved, when she was twelve, to help out on the farm and in the care of her younger siblings. This was common in early twentieth century Irish agricultural communities. The boys in the family would help their father with the heavier farming chores or with cutting, drying and stacking the turf from the peat bog; this would be used year round to fuel the fireplace for cooking and for heating their two-room, slate-floored home with a thatched roof. The girls would sometimes be sent to town to work, as was my mother when she was fourteen. All the children would be expected to leave home before eighteen to find jobs elsewhere and send money home. My grandparents' farm was too small and the soil too unyielding to feed many adults. This was true for many of the rural areas in western Ireland in the province of Connaught. The impoverishment of this province was once summed up in the seventeenth century by Oliver Cromwell's curse: "To Hell or Connaught!"

Kiltyclogher was not only poor, but also had the bad luck of being on the border of Northern Ireland. In July, on "bonfire night," my mother and her siblings would steal out after dark to their farm's "white hill," named for the flowers that bloomed there all summer. With a mixture of excitement and fear, they would watch the fires in the valley to the North. They didn't know that "bonfire night" signified the beginning of the Protestant celebration of the defeat of Catholic James II by William of Orange in 1690. The children knew only that the fires meant they were hated by the Protestants.

Since the shop where my mother worked was four miles from her family's farm in an area called Raheelin, she stayed most of the time at the McGowans' home in town. But she missed her parents and nine brothers and sisters. Her father would come to pick up her pay every week, and rarely invited her home for a visit. Margaret knew it was expected that she turn over her earnings to help out the family, but was hurt by her father's coldness. Realizing he was not forbidding her to come home, she occasionally borrowed a bicycle or walked the badly-rutted road to visit her mother and siblings.

After the encounter with the Black and Tans my mother knew she wanted to leave Ireland. She went to nearby Manorhamilton to see her older married sister Honora, better known as Annie. For the next two years, they plotted Margaret's departure. Annie saved the classified ads from the newspaper and together they pored over them, searching out employment possibilities for my mother. Finally, at sixteen, without telling her parents, she decided to leave. An enticing job as a live-in housekeeper was waiting for her in Birmingham, England. Getting into that country would not present a problem for a young Irish lass. Ireland was still a colony of England; thus my mother was a British subject and entitled to enter and work there. Irish lads, however, did not have such ease of access. They were carefully screened for possible IRA connections.

For a girl who had never traveled beyond the hills of Leitrim, going to England was a courageous step. My mother saw it as thrilling, as she often viewed novel or risky situations in her life.

Annie helped her pack a bag and gave her money and a roasted chicken, wrapped in newspaper, to tide her over on the long trip. Margaret first had to traverse Ireland by train to the east coast and Dublin, on to the port of Dunleary for the boat to Holyhead, Wales, and then a train to England. My mother, having a tendency to dramatize, described the crossing as so rough that the cuspidor on the floor spun clear across the ceiling and back to the deck, several times.

Excited and anxious on her arrival at the home in which she would work, she was immediately put at ease by the woman of the house, and shown to her room. Her own room! Margaret easily learned her tasks and was delighted to be there. The family liked her too, and showed her around the city. She met up with other young Irish people in the area and went to church and dances with them. She loved the family she worked for and enjoyed her new friends and her life in Birmingham. My mother was happy and thought she would stay there forever. In the meantime she made peace with her parents and sent home all the money she could.

Abruptly one day she received a letter from her father commanding her to come home. She was to go with her younger sister Bessie to America. Amidst tears she left the wonderful life she had made for herself in England. "I had to obey my father," she told me many years later.

The country Margaret returned to was very different from the one she had left five years earlier. The British occupation was over, the *Irish Free State* was officially proclaimed and its boundary with Northern Ireland fixed. Yet the poverty of her parents' farm remained the same. All the money my mother had been sending home was being used to send one or more of her siblings to America. Her brothers Frank and Pat were already in New York. She was glad she didn't have to stay home on the farm.

In 1926 my mother and Bessie left Leitrim, traveling east to Cork and the port of Cobh for their ship to New York. On board, they met other Irish youngsters, some of whom had fiddles, pennywhistles and harmonicas. One even had an accordion. Anywhere there was music and dancing, Margaret joined in. While jigging and singing with her fellow émigrés, she could forget her sadness at leaving home once again. My mother always loved a party, and she and her compatriots knew how to throw one in the tight space of their steerage class cabins and decks.

Margaret and Bessie joined their brothers in New York and began looking for work. My mother soon got a position as live-in housekeeper with the family of a Jewish doctor in Flatbush, Brooklyn. Again she loved her job and the family, and they loved her. She grew to like New York even more than Birmingham, especially after she met my father, Patrick Donnellan. They married, settled down in Brooklyn and raised my five siblings and me.

A few of my cousins still live on the old farm in Kiltyclogher raising cattle. Ireland's participation in the European Union has helped farmers find markets for their butter and meat. The old thatched cottage has become a barn with a tin roof, and a small but comfortable four room farmhouse was built in the 1960's. More recently the area has become a favorite spot for Continental Europeans to build vacation homes, and a right of way has been cut through my grandparents' property. The "troubles" from 1969 to the 1990's have mainly ceased and the borders between the North and the Republic of Ireland have re-opened, facilitating commerce. Kiltyclogher is a busier but more peaceful village now.

DAD
Brian Leong, Age 7

1. My Dad is strong.
2. My Dad watches T.V. everyday in the morning.
3. He is very smart.
4. He helps me do my homework.
5. He is tall.
6. He plays games with me.
7. He loves to sleep.
8. He loves to play games with me.
9. He is a little coo-coo.
10. He watches T.V. at night.

THE VESSEL FILLERS
Marietta Mason

It was a beautiful Monday morning. The sun was shining very brightly, as if it was trying to make amends for the brutal winds and bone chilling temperatures that we had so recently endured. I was on my way to a ten o'clock routine appointment with my ophthalmologist. I was missing my Tai Chi class which was also at ten Monday mornings. I would ask for another day in the week when scheduling my next visit, to avoid a conflict. As I made my way carefully down the three steps leading into the office, my ears were alerted to the sound of someone talking in a loud voice.

When I opened the door my hearing was beyond alerted; it was assaulted by the voice of a woman speaking at an above-conversational volume. Vulgar, caustic utterances spilled from her mouth like the rotten contents of an overturned garbage can. She seasoned her verbal onslaught with a four letter word she seemed comfortable with using over and over again. The waiting room was filled with patients, and five staff members were in the reception area. The presence of others did not deter the woman; in fact her voice became louder. She kept shouting that she didn't care about the referral forms that she needed in order for the doctor to see her daughter. She wasn't missing another day of work for nothing, and she wasn't leaving without seeing him.

Suddenly the doctor came out of his office and approached the ranting woman. He spoke to her in a calm but firm voice. He explained (as his staff had done earlier) that he would not be able to see her daughter without the proper forms. She continued shouting and cursing, hardly pausing to breathe. The doctor then tried to appeal to any ember of decency smoldering within the woman's combustible behavior. He told her she was embarrassing herself and her child, and she should stop. The doctor's statement heightened her anger and her determination to get her way. She continued to scream and curse. The doctor (still remaining calm but firm) asked her to leave the office and never return. The woman turned abruptly and with a violent movement of her hand swept everything that was on the reception desk off onto the floor. She then pushed the door open and went out, followed quickly by a girl who I think was about six or seven years old. The patients in the room reacted as if they all had just awakened from the same bad dream. They slowly began to pick up candy, candy dish, magazines, business cards, and the sign-in sheets that were littering the floor. They returned those items to the desk and went back to their seats. The receptionist also seemed to awaken, saw me standing in front of her, asked my name and which doctor I had come to see. She told me to sign in. I signed the sheet and took a seat among my fellow patients, who were beginning to talk about what they had so recently witnessed. They spoke in quiet voices almost as if they thought the violent woman would come back if they talked too loudly.

My doctor (who shares the office with a colleague) was not aware of the earlier disturbance. I filled him in on the morning's event and asked if they had any security. He said all they could do when something of that nature occurred was to call 911.

After my examination, I stopped at the desk to schedule my next appointment, asking for a day besides Monday so it wouldn't conflict with my Tai Chi class. The receptionist looked at me with a disbelieving smile, perhaps doubting that I could be a student of a martial art. Looking straight at her I said in a perky voice, "You guys could have used my skills earlier today." My statement made both of us laugh, and she playfully agreed that they could have used my help.

I left the office and walked to the bus stop where I was joined by a woman with two small girls. I was drawn to their conversation. One girl asked, "Mom, what does donate mean? My teacher wants us to donate shoes, donate coats, donate dresses, and other stuff for kids that need them."

Her mother explained that to donate meant to give something to someone who didn't have what they needed, and didn't have a way or money to get things for themselves. She also told her child that it was good to share with others that weren't as fortunate as she was. The girl seemed satisfied with her mother's answer and added that she would donate some toys for the kids. Her mother told her it was a nice idea.

The bus arrived, we all got on, and I was no longer able to hear any further exchange between mother and daughter. As I rode along on the way home my thoughts turned to the two events that had taken place that day and the vivid differences in each one. I found myself imagining that the girls in the two events were vessels and that their mothers were Vessel Fillers. One mother had chosen to fill her vessel with angry language, disrespect for self and others, lawlessness and violence. While the other mother had chosen to fill her vessel with helpful knowledge, compassion for others and the value of sharing with those less fortunate than she was. My mind took a look into the distant future when the girls would become women and perhaps be blessed with their own vessels. I wondered, how would they choose to fill them?

WHEN
Michelle Broady

When a baby's cry who's there
to hold him?

When a baby's fall who's there
to catch him?

When a baby's happy who's there
to share it with him?

When a baby's sad who's there
to comfort him?

Only I can cause
I'm his mother.

FERRIS WHEEL
Dwight Smith

My sister went to sigh
As she went to the carnival
And blew balloons
And spent money
On the Ferris Wheel

TONY
Kim Storms

My son, I am so very proud of you. You are a very precious gift from God, that I am learning to respect and love more and more each day.

I glow with excitement knowing it's time to visit you.

My hair, my clothes, my smile, they all have to be just right.

My heart is jumping, my brain is high, I'm a little over the border of hysteria, because you, your handsome face, your manly posture, that gorgeous smile, take my breath, with one glimpse of you.

The joy and all the overwhelming feelings I go through when the time is near, have only one explanation…

I love you.

MOM
Virdah Zaman, Age 14

My mommy is da best.
She smells good
Well dats what I think!!
My mommy is da best.
She takes me places
And make da best food.
My mommy is da best.
She hates sweets
For some stupid reason.
My mommy is da best.
A one-of-kind
Dats why my
        MOMmy is da BEST!

ANIYA IMANI
Lisa Washington

My daughter—Aniya Imani—she is two years old
and
BAD as HELL.
Trying to do everything
on her own…
walking, playing, yelling.
She thinks she's twenty-one.
Soon I'll be twenty-one.
That means I'll be legal—legal for anything.
That means I have to start being more responsible
for my own doings.
The light of my eyes—Aniya Imani.
The two-year-old that thinks she's grown.
The little girl that laughs, plays, giggles, cries,
and asks,
"Mommy are you ok?"
When she cries…I cry.
When she laughs…I laugh.
When she plays…I play.
My baby girl.

A FARAWAY GIFT
Myra Baum

A large wool shawl
Red paisley print
On pale yellow background
Long lush fringes
Layer of warmth
And beauty
Sheltering shoulders.

Traveled from Russia
In son's suitcase
Returning from
Junior year abroad
Anchored in England
Study trip to Russia.

All this traveling
From a boy
Who hated
Sleep-away camp

Sent home
Drawing
Of child's face
With wrinkles

Caption read:
"Am getting old here,
Come get me."

I SHALL DOTE MYSELF

I SHALL DOTE MYSELF
Almedia S. Knight

I was inspired to write "I Shall Dote Myself" Mother's Day, after noticing I had not received one card from my four (4) children! Perhaps they cannot—after so many Mother's Days—find the right words to express their sentiments. Here, my children, I Shall Dote Myself.

I am a widow, mother, grandmother and great-grandmother,
a sister, partner and friend—
just an ordinary woman who can do extraordinary things.
I know how to lead, and
I can follow
I am naïve:
        shun sophistication in styles and techniques
I am ingenious:
        clever, original, and effective.
I am sensitive, but
        can be thick-skinned
I am a pragmatic, yet
I have fancies:
        impulsiveness, desirous—sometimes unfounded.

I'd rather truthful pains than comforting lies
I try not to judge, for
I too may be judged
I like goodness,
I dislike wickedness…
        I see me in both.

I witness justice and experience its prejudice
I practice tolerance, and
I disavow unpermissiveness
I see love as a present and
        give it wholeheartedly.

I, myself, believe:
  love, loyalty, and honor to be precursors…
    to gently tapping the souls of humanity
      to bring out the best
        of humankind…what I believe
          can be a cure for the worst conditions.

RECIPE FOR SHUNN
Shunn Theingi, Age 11

One million bowls of smart big brain
One bowl of brave mind
Ten teaspoons of sensible and attractive mind
One pair of eyeballs (two)
One bowl of beauty smile
One bowl of smart and intelligence brain
One bowl of Chinese
One bowl of dark black long hair
One bowl of friendly mind
One bowl of kindness and helpful mind
One bowl of adventurous
One bowl of beautiful teeth
One bowl of cute face (included nose and everything)
Put them from head to toes
That will make a good fine
Shunn

UNTITLED
(LOOKING AT PHOTOGRAPHS OF FACES)
Qiiyana Simpkins, Age 17

    My life was always a mystery to my family and friends. One minute I'd be this very shy timid person always hiding my face from the world. I'd go from that to being sweet and innocent. But don't let my looks fool or deceive you, I can be highly upset the next minute, or look like death before your eyes. I can hide behind a lot of makeup and fancy clothes, but when the makeup comes off you can see my life stories through all of the art on my body. Or my life stories and pain could be hidden behind laughs and smiles. Be careful while laughing, though. You might upset the dogs or frighten the people around you. Or, I could have no emotion, always having a blank expression. My name could be anything you want it to be.

MY NAME
Brian Leong, Age 7

My name is Brian Leong.
It sounds like all long.
It tastes like mangos.
It is the color of gold and silver.
It reminds me of a flower called a black rose.
It means "I am strong."
I like my name because it has an "L" at the end of Brian.

I THINK NOT
Jacqueline Murray

I think not of my five foot three stature
as I watch the fashion glide
I think not of my rounded hipline
or my bust on its downward slide.

I glare at the stick thin figures
as they parade their slinky gowns
As flash bulbs pop and capture them
as they sport their shaky crowns.

I proudly hoist my bosoms up
and take a low heeled stride.
The height of heel means nothing
my heart is filled with pride.

No envious thoughts invade my brain
while runway models are raising Cain.
Am I any less beautiful, any less vain?
I think not.

BECAUSE
Mikhal Morris, Age 11

Because the sky is blue,
My favorite color is blue.

Because he's eating pizza,
I want pizza.

Because she writes "love,"
I must write love too.

Because she is bad,
I must act bad too.

Because because is because
Because is my because.

THE HISTORY IN ME
Najaya Royal, age 10

The History in me makes me who I am! I see Rosa Parks in me when I am tired and sleepy sitting in the bus to be more clear in the front of the bus. I see Dr. King when I get out of school saying, "Thank God I am free at last." I see Harriet Tubman in me when I help people where they want to be. Then finally, I see me yes me being those 3 powerful people all in one, being a 1-person band playing 3 instruments together.

The new person I see in History Is Me!

DEAR NOSE
Justina Jordan

You get a lot of attention because you are small.
People love to touch you.
I wonder where I got the dent? I wonder if it came from
	pressing it while
playing because I loved to look at Tabitha on TV
Because none of my parents have this nose.
So mine is unique
Because I probably got it from one of my ancestors.

I AM A CAR
Marie Anicet, Age 16

I am a car.
I'm fast.
Seven cylinders of speed.
I break down at times,
but if you take care of me,
I'll last you a lifetime.

I USED TO
Bridin McCann, Age 6

I didn't cry so much,
But now I do.

I used to play dress-up,
But now I don't.

I used to play kitchen a lot,
But now I don't.

My mom used to wear make-up,
But now she does not.

LOOK UP
Donna M. Dickerson

My life has had its ups and downs,
Been through loads of villages and towns.

I am so happy to know that I changed today,
From silence to a woman with lots to say.

A woman, mother and lover of life am I,
Now at night I'm amazed when I look up at the sky.

THE RIGHT FIT
Jacqueline Murray

The right fit seems to have eluded me for the past fifteen years.

I used to enjoy shopping, trying on clothes, and tipping around in three inch heels. No more. The problem seems to be that I'm allergic to food. Whenever I eat, I break out in fat.

This allergy has affected me from head to toe. My boobs seem to pop out of even the larger sized bras. I graduated from a "C" cup to a "DD." I thought I had solved the problem, but now when I look in the mirror I think I have three protrusions there instead of two.

There was a time I wore size 9 panty. Then the seams began to split, so I went to size 10. So far, so good.

I have given up on pantyhose, because size XL seems to ease its way down my hips, and ends up around my knees.

I just buy ankle highs now. Thigh highs cut the circulation in my legs.

At one time I sauntered around in size 7 narrow shoes, but after wearing flat nurse's shoes for years, I have gone to 9 medium, and they gap on the sides.

Being short compounds the problem. Pants that fit don't always come in short and dresses that fit are way too long.

I'm beginning to feel unloved and unappreciated. Anyone know a good seamstress?

WHERE I AM FROM
Shaquanna Cole

I am from the rich tribes of Africa
where pharaohs and queens ruled their land.
I am from gold jewels created
in Africa.
Where hunters wore tribal colors
and provided for their family.
I am from a culture where leaders
died for a cause.
Where Martin led people to equality.
Where Madame C.J. Walker became the first self-made
woman millionaire.
Where am I from?
From the deepest hopes of a slave
that one day freedom would be.

I AM
Somayah Aljahmi, Age 12

I am the green melookiah, or Arabic spinach.
I am a yellow camel in the desert.
I am watermelon Jolly Ranchers.
I am the cold,
frosty,
and beautiful winter
when the trees are naked and the streets are white.

I am a convertible.
I am "We Can Work It Out" and Jupiter from "The Planets."
I am the sunny day after a long week of rain.
I am happiness and joy.

I am a sea-shell,
left behind because the hermit crab grew out,
and waiting to be found by another.

I am the time I got the letter from Hunter.
And how I didn't pass the test.
And how I didn't make it because I wasn't better than someone else.
And how I couldn't go to Manhattan every day,
to and from school,
and wake up every day at five.

I am the blow horn that hides the words of another,
as the other leaves out to the depths of the sea,
living on the quiet sound of the whales and ocean,
but dies from loneliness

I am the green netted silk that my older sister's henna dress
is made out of.

IS THIS ALL REAL?

LOOKING OUT OF THE WINDOW
Lorraine Beyer Theordor

On 35th Street in Coney Island, watching the boys
on roller skates hanging on to the back of the trolley
car, for a fun free ride.

To the left, the beach called to me until it was too cold,
and when it was so cold, we were building fortresses
from mountains of snow.

I thought the world was mostly Jewish then,
except for James Cagney, Pat O'Brien and Spencer Tracy.

Up and down the street, from every open window, no TV,
no AC then, you could hear the radios shouting the
grace of the brown bomber, Joe Louis.

And then we moved to Sheepshead Bay, where I found
adventure in Greek, Irish and Italian friendships.

Now I look out of the window, on top of Virgin Records
and Circuit City, overlooking Union Square Park.
I see a colorful, scrambling world and I ask…
Is this all real?

I AM FROM THE GHETTO
Malik Garnett, Age 12

I am from the ghetto
This is my home
This is my story
True ghetto story
This is my story
Real ghetto story
The ghetto is where you hear
The bullets and trains
Where you hear the screams and the rains
This is where people get shot
99 bullets straight up on the block
People lose families
People lose daddys
People lose mommies
People always cryin'
This is the pain
We are really in vain
I want this to stop
When I grow up I am going to walk
Straight up on that block
I am going to say
This is my story
True ghetto story
This is my story
Real ghetto story.

OUT MY WINDOW
Basma Azzamok, Age 7

When I look out my window I see
lots of cars rushing through the street
a small roof top and cars to buy
a Dish building
and houses from East of my apartment building
and a sign PathMark that's red and blue
and this is what I see out my window

EASTER
Carlos Garcia

Easter is coming
so you see everybody preparing themselves
on what they are going to wear.

Air Force 1's sell out in stores
green money shirts for the guys
pink for the girls or white
and baby blue for both.

I went shopping for mine outfit already with the guys from my block
just waitin' for one of the many days that everybody outside shines.

HOME AT LAST
Paul Francois, Age 11

I went from the east to the west looking for my home. I climbed up onomatopoeia walked through simile and crossed metaphor until I reached my destination. Oh Boy! It is good to be home. Even though it took a while, I survived and lived through all the obstacles that made me stumble. I ran like the wind seeing my house a mile away. I was panting when I reached it.

At last.

Home at last!

BLINDING
Jolee Cohen, Age 10

As I walk in,
I notice the lights,
almost blinding my eyes.
So I look down
to the floor.
Seeing the reflection
almost as blinding
as the lights by
themselves.
I just close my eyes,
thinking I can see
the lights through
my eyelids. I just
walk away, thinking
why did I walk into that
room in the first place?

HOT DAY IN BROOKLYN
Myra Baum

Sweltering sidewalks signal
Beach Day.
Sandwiches sealed in wax paper
Dressed in bathing suits
Hidden by shorts and skirts
We trek to train.

Doors open
Squeeze in
Stand body to body
Subway sways

Kids giggle
Face pressed to window
Seeking sand and surf
Suddenly, the smell
Of salt water fills the air
This is it.
Brighton Beach Station.

Two blocks to beach
Then hot sand
Burns our feet
As we search for
The perfect spot

Spread blanket
Anchored by shoes
One in each corner

Race to water's edge
Plop down

Build seaside mansions
Dribble, dribble, dribble
Drops of wet sand
One upon the other
Castles slowly appear
And then disappear

Temporary housing
Washed away
By waves.

MY BLOCK
Carlos Garcia

On my block
everybody gets along
we are all united.

On my block
graffiti is very important
because the guys from my block run de city.

On my block
everybody is a sneakers fan.
We all collect sneakers throughout the winter
to wear them in the summer time.

On my block
the whole year looks like summer time.

IL MONDE IN THE PROFANE
Pat Jackson

Inner city street,
it's hot and humid and someone thinks he's el Cid

Inner city street,
with neon bare-bulbs blinking,
garbage cans stinking

Inner city street,
hear its rhythmic be-bop talk,
hidden muggers stalk

Inner city street,
practicing karate chops
in squat little shops

Inner city street,
junkies at curbside reeling,
at last unfeeling

Inner city street,
massage parlor marquee and
garish graffiti

Inner city street,
unemployed men daring time,
wicked women chime

Inner city street,
with your litter lying limp,
where's your pretty pimp?

Inner city street,
boozed bums smacking on their gums,
hearing soundless drums

Inner city street,
what are these sins you extol
with your shameful soul?

Inner city street,
Il monde in the profane,
from sane to insane

WHAT'S NEXT?
Mattie Livingstone

Maybella drive, as if to be blind
They sing loud, maybe not listening
The baby is crying, need a bottle
Come home not too late in the morning
I am hungry, do not want to eat
My brother moved, not out of town
The girls went to dance. The boys are at home
My mother birthday today. The party next week
It cold outside, no clothes on

BLUE SKY
Justina Jordan

I woke up today and saw the beautiful sunshine
And the blue sky with clouds
I saw a little girl wearing pink
And the snow still on the ground

I smell tobacco
I smell perfume
I smell coffee
I smell the cats

I heard the birds sing a nice melody
While I sat on the bench and smoked a cigarette
I hear the men working on a building and it's coming out
really nice

HAIKU FOR SPRING
Carole Beaubien Gregory

1
New green leaves come out,
my identity in trees—
a sacred brown trunk.

2
We are brown & live,
infinity's language
grows the green of leaves.

3
At the park I see,
green languages sing all day—
Spring sacredly is.

4
Flowing green the trees
dance in the wind's songs—
I wildly join their sweet sounds.

5
Purple tulips stand,
white tulips turn up to sun—
their green stems hold all.

6
Pigeons follow work,
Perhaps hands will toss bread—
pigeons peck peck Earth.

MAGICAL ROOM
Nancy Beck

The room was magical. The room was mine and mine alone. In this room I could stay up all night, a vigil, listening to the sounds of the house, the street, watching the mockingbird dance in a tree while it sang in summer, or watching the cars crunch through the snow after a winter storm.

But mostly to watch for the bomb that might fall, hoping to see it coming so I could wake everyone to get to the basement in time. To keep us safe.

The room had a closet, not wide, but very deep. I could go in there, behind the hanging clothes, a secret place. Too dark to play, but a place to keep…secret anyway.

The window looked out next to a sloping part of the road. I could imagine slipping out the window, sliding down the roof, hanging from the gutter by my hands 'til the distance to the ground was not so great. I could make my escape.

GHETTO
Najaya Royal, age 10

Gone

Horrible

Evil

Terrible

Terrifying

Awfully bad

These, these words tell, tell us what the G.H.E.T.T.O is all about. If you moved to where I live you made a terrible, terrifying, awfully bad move. But, wel- welcome to the bloody, to the bloody, Ghetto. But don't worry, worry, worry, because something, something, something good is gonna come for us!

SOUNDS
Veronika Antoniadis, Age 13

The soft whisper of a bird's wings. A silent
ruffle of a light-footed cat's tail. The cry
of a baby who's dropped his pacifier,
the loud beats of a drummer's song. The
river's low lullaby as it flows south. A
screamo band screams their lyrics and
pumps the crowd. The sweet melody of
a guitarist's notes linger in the air
even after the notes died out. The moon,
a silver orb in the night sky, says nothing,
yet murmurs it all in the dark.

UNTITLED
Jenny Lynn Adames

I see posters on the wall with crazy colors and shit
a tornado flying by looking like
a ice crusher damaging the
streets and the baseball
field just got a face
lift

MARY KATHRYN'S BELIEFS

MARY KATHRYN'S BELIEFS
Mary Kate Tramontano, Age 6

I Believe in:

God
Jesus
Fairies
Mermaids
Myself
All people
Little people
Nice people
Spiderman

I Do Not Believe in:

Batman
Bad People
Mean People
Superman

I don't believe in anything else.

WHAT MONEY CAN'T BUY
Shirley N. Bland

I am redeemed, but not with silver
I am bought, but not with gold
Bought with a price—the blood of Jesus
Precious price of love untold

I'd rather walk in the dark with God
Than go alone in the light
I'd rather walk by faith with Him
We walk by faith, not by sight
Where God guides, He provides

JANUARY'S END
Michael Cook

Writing hieroglyphics on clouds,
Remembering shared skies
And massive stones
Gathered in large circles and shapes
From lifetimes ago,
Consecrated to ancient, ancestral memories
In a planetary galaxy beyond us;
Scratching at meaning in this world, in the sand,
As we've done since time immemorial,
In vapors and on cave walls in this dimension,
Only recently unearthing beings
Who built Stonehenge, 4600 years ago;
Watching the world move forward from that point,
Wherever we are, whoever we are now, as a species,
Transcribing what comes from the skies
And the fields left for us to plow, allowing sustenance,
Of what we're here on earth to learn….

It seems so convulsively absurd
Yet simultaneously appropriate;
So much is cathartic in this breath, on earth,
In its resonance, now….

This is the point I've gotten to:
Writing notes to eternity, making lists on clouds,
Trying to take into consideration
Everything that's gone before us,
Maybe everything that IS….

THANKS
Linda Thomas

When you get up in the morning
    Thank God
When you're given another chance
      to make things right
Thank God
When someone says hello
    that you don't know
When the pain subsides
Thank God
When a child smiles or a baby cries
When the trees change their clothes
A wind blows
The sun shines
The water is cool
The argument is forgotten
The hurt stops
You think you're alone
Then you hear a song a psalm
You laugh
Thank God
You have a place to call home
You have change to give the homeless
You cry with joy
Thank God

I THOUGHT I SAW GOD
Frances Buschke

I thought I saw God the other day
Indescribable, which leaves me with no poem
Ever since I was a child, which I still am
      I have seen the most awesome things in nature
Sunsets, morning clouds bleeding red into a darkening sea
The blackness of night, with the velvety sea rolling in the background
A seductress
The ice glaciers cooling in Alaska
      Swiftly moving towards them in a boat, silently gliding
      to an even greater silence
My whole body is electric, shaking inside
I am all, I am nothing, I am a part of all this
Every particle of me is inside every particle outside me
      in these moments
In New Mexico my body knew a stork was sailing in
      long before it arrived, gray and green light, tumultuous,
      like an animal, a dog, that other sense knowing
In all this I thought I saw God
I don't know what God is
But I thought I saw some immense Power, beyond thought,
      words. It was only feeling and non feeling.
I thought I saw…

LUIGI ALMOST BROKE MY CELL PHONE

LUIGI ALMOST BROKE MY CELL PHONE
Marilyn Solares, Age 12

My Luigi almost broke my cell phone, my cell phone.
My sweetheart almost did, yes, yes.
I took a picture and he almost broke it, yes, yes.
I love him, yes, yes.

BROKEN THINGS WANT
Barry Blitstein

Broken things want whole things STOP I want broken things whole STOP I love whole things broken STOP broken things love whole things STOP broken love wants things whole STOP I want broken love whole STOP whole love wants broken things STOP things I want broken love whole things STOP whole things love broken things BUT things broken want whole love
                            I,
                       broken,
                  BUT WANT
                      love
                      whole

NINE WAYS OF LOOKING AT HIM
Genesis Niara Lee

As he walks behind you
Take a glance over your shoulder.
There you would see this enchanting figure.

The noise you hear
That's not wanted around
As you turn to your right, it's him

Watching love and basketball
As the quarters pass by.
The old songs are blasting
And you hear him
Singing along.

As you go to the bathroom
He is who you'll pass by

Listening to rap music
On the radio loud
Would be him and his homeboy

Deep sensual voices
You'll hear them, really loud
A conversation which he is having
But you wouldn't guess with whom

The eyes that you feel
As you turn would be his

The smirk on his face
That when you look at him turns,
It turns into the biggest smile you've ever seen

The one that you're staring at
And the one who stares back

FIRST LOVE
Allen Hoage

I was in love in junior high school and her name was Diane. She wore glasses and dressed very nice. We were in the eighth grade and I loved her; she felt the same way about me also. We never went out for a walk or to the park.

Sometimes I see her brother and I ask him, "How is Diane doing?" He says, "She is all right."

"Tell her I ask about her," I say.

He says, "I will tell her."

SHE WAS MY PROJECT
Van Everkool

Okay, so she was fifty years old...You know the average starship is supposed to be good for at least a buck fifty, right?

When first I laid eyes on her, the windows on her cockpit seemed to light up; yes they definitely had a shine.

Her fuselage was a little dented, hinting at her age, but her sleek curves and subtle contours suggested a much younger model.

I decided at once that I had to have her. Whether she functioned properly, hell even if she needed a total overhaul, I had to make her mine. The first thing I did was attempt to access her onboard computer. There were several security protocols in place, undoubtedly put there by her previous pilot. Some were redundant, unnecessary; others let me know that she had traveled through dangerous territory, that there had been a fear of viral infection or being pirated.

After a while, I was able to comprehend the security codes, thus gaining access to the systems and navigation section of her mainframe. It immediately became apparent that she was just as seductively beautiful inside as she was out.

She had some damage, it's true, especially with her navigational programs. I was confident that my prowess, patience, persistence, would restore her to her former glory, to performing like a showroom model of the present.

The first time I tried to initiate her primary booster, I failed. This was undoubtedly due to atrophy; she hadn't been boarded in years after all.

Carefully, methodically, lovingly, I coaxed her engines from warm to red-hot. She quivered, shuttered, then began to purr. Finally my patience paid off. I was able to jump-start her power core to activate her stardrive. She was even more magnificent than I had anticipated. She ascended through the atmosphere like a missile. We achieved the heavens faster than I had with any other vessel. We were soaring through the stars! When she reached her full potential, it seemed as if we were one entity, moving through time and space at the speed of thought. Total satisfaction had been achieved on many levels.

BC CHARM
Precious Wilson

If I were in a different time
I would be the most charming person
too?

Every word would compliment
your beauty. With a smile
your wish is my command.

Your strength is my weakness.
Your weakness is my strength.
There would be no time to stop thinking of me.

I can make anyone smile
each time we meet
present or not.

When that perfect moment comes
I wrote the book—on
supply and demand.

UNTITLED
Raquel Hill

can you please marry me
I picked out some rings for you
and I thought about it but I wasn't
sure which one you'd like so I
bought you eight diamonds and
a plain wedding band so you
can create your own
you're beautiful and I want
you to have the best ring in the
world and I'm pretty sure you
wouldn't want any other girl to
have your ring

maybe you'll make a
crazy style then millions
of people would want to
put it on their display
and we could name the
ring Eight Beautiful Things
doesn't that sound great

wait a second you still
haven't told me my answer
so what's it going to
be yes or no

ODE TO ELTON
Dyane L. Miller

I'm a city girl. Born and bred in Harlem. At the age of twenty-seven, I finally grew tired of the New York hustle and bustle. My first boyfriend, Elton, was from Rocky Mount, North Carolina, and since our first late night walk together, hand in hand, he filled my head with wonderful thoughts of living closer to God. So I packed a duffle and cashed in my ticket to Asheville.

The mountains were overwhelming, the stars breathtaking. I learned so much living in Sylvia, near Asheville. Like at dusk, bats by the multitudes flew out of their resting place and gathered near my home. It was amazing to leave my door open, screen door closed, and hear a bear moan in the distant hills. Or see a mountain lion walk down Main Street in broad daylight. Or to find out a certain frog lives in trees. Or to simply lie in my yard, looking up into the galaxies and suddenly know how ants feel.

Living in the mountains I took notice that the hills were shaped like the breasts of women…Nature at her best. For ten years, I walked close with God, an experience I will always attribute to my first love, Elton.

SPRING TIME IS MY TIME
Ruby Ellerbe Scott

I love the spring time, and who doesn't
A time of rebirth of renewal of regeneration
The grass returns to its chlorophyllic colors
The flowers take the chance
and with courage they bud preparing to bloom
The trees re-dress starting with tiny leaflets
that soon cover their naked branches
The sky blushes with blue that warms the heart
chasing the grey away
I love the spring, spring time is my time

Spring is the time for redecoration
new declarations and exciting preparations
Down come the heavy drapes
to be replaced with the fluttering curtains
Windows are cleaned to welcome the view
and the bright morning sun
Old rugs are tossed and floors shine with wax
Heavy coats return to their place of storage
making room for outfits of color galore
Boots and oxfords hidden for a time
as toeless sandals and slides happily take their place
I love the spring, spring time is my time

New relations are made from your walk in the park
or the smile in your eyes
Our view of each other is clearer
because of our personal rebirth
Toe nails cut, hair is groomed

attention to looks a totally different thing
We're bouncing in the sunshine
matching our stride to the sounds of nature
But best of all is the budding of a new love
that blooms into a summer romance
Can't beat it, spring time, a time of rebirth
renewal, regeneration and preparation
I love the spring, spring time is my time

TRYING TO GET EVEN

TRYING TO GET EVEN
Bob Rosen

Matty dozed off and the shouts of the men screaming at the closed circuit TV set overhead woke him up. It wasn't enough for those losers to come out to the track to see their money disappear before their eyes. No, they had to keep the action going between live races by trying to beat the odds at a racetrack hundreds of miles away, somewhere hopefully where it was sunnier than the grim skies over Queens. It hadn't always been like this, he thought, remembering the times before he lost his job, when he would head straight to the clubhouse just to avoid this riffraff. He and his pal Phil would come out at least twice during the week, besides making the Big A their weekend home.

Phil's brother was a well-connected union delegate who brought him into his local. Phil had been on the union books for years. After all, if family can't do for you, then who could? Matty became his buddy after coming to his rescue at the big A. Phil had cashed a big winning ticket; this was when Angel Cordero was winning everything in sight. You could put him on a three-legged piece of garbage and he'd be there at the end waving his whip overhead past the finish line. I don't know how those jockeys take all the crap that gets thrown at them from the bettors—"Angel, you bastard, your old lady's a big *puta*. I need this winner or else."—You know, stuff like that. Well, Phil had a bundle of cash in his pocket and now he needed to take a leak. Matty saw two guys with dreadlocks follow him into the toilet and just knew they were meaning to kick the crap out of him. They started, but Matty was Johnny on the spot.

"I may be lazy, but I'm no chickenshit," Matty thought about those days. I crack one guy's head into the other monkey's noggin, and out they fly. Now I'm Phil's friend for life. So now it's me and Philly, union brothers. Oh sure, once in a while I had to do some real work. After all, there's just so much his brother could do for me."

"Boy, what a feeling it was." Phil would drive him to the track. Phil had just gotten his brother's Cadillac from the union bosses. It was last year's model; his brother, the big shot, got a brand new DeVille, bright red with a tan roof. Phil had given the union boss a tip on a long shot, something like twenty-five to one, and he made a killing. Well, he made a bundle; you didn't say *killing* around the union hall. That's how he was riding first class with his buddy right up to the valet parking lane. Some days they came out ahead, but to be honest, most of the time they stunk up the place. The trainers made sure never to be seen talking to Phil because his brother had his name in the papers whenever some nosey reporter needed a mob story to fill up the columns. Matty hung out with the guys near the backstretch barns. All they could tell him was which of their horses didn't stand a chance. If they warned him off a nag and it won at a big price, he used to twist their ears until they screamed, "Let go!" It was a tough way to make a living.

One night around the Fourth of July a full moon and the offshore breezes siphoned off the water from the shoreline around the Bergen Beach marshes along the Belt Parkway. Among the rusted auto chassis a man's body, fully clothed, turned up, decorated with seaweed, tiny fiddler crabs, and a bullet hole in the temple. The NY Post had been running a series about Croatian mobsters trying to muscle in on the trade unions. This big shot wannabe must have stepped on too many toes once too often.

Every law enforcement agency wanted a piece of this story, and the Feds took control of the investigation. You could make your reputation as the lead investigator on a juicy story about mob influence, and then you could run for mayor of New York City. It's happened before. The FBI threw out a fishing line and hooked into a connection between the murder and mob influence in the construction union. The wind up was Phil's brother's local had provided the muscle to get rid of the Croat thug. The government took over the local, and that was the end of Phil's and Matty's free ride, and all the favors that came with being on the inside.

Now, Matty took the A train out to the track on days when he could sit in the grandstand without freezing to death. "If the globe is warming, it sure isn't out here in this part of Queens," he thought to himself. Young people didn't come out here much, or as a matter of fact, neither did the old timers. Too many distractions now, and there was talk that the only way to save the sport was to put in video gambling machines. He was pinching pennies now, looking to turn ten bucks into a big ticket, and would always bet on a horse with Annie in its name. That was his Mom's name.

"I took her out to the track once, and we lost the first three races," he reminded himself.

"Matty, this is what you do for fun?" she'd said. "Look at these men here moping on the benches. Their shoes are ripped and their coats are ready for the garbage can. You have to straighten your life out." She picked herself up and headed for the exit. He never took her again.

This morning he felt different about his chances. The young guy on the first floor in his building came up with the twenty bucks he had promised to pay him for sitting in his car until ten-thirty in the morning a couple of days a week. That was when the sweepers cleaned the curb. You had better move or risk getting a parking ticket for at least eighty dollars. If a tow truck came along and hooked you up you were looking at two hundred bucks, cash money, and a trip over to the west side storage yard. The guys that ran that place looked like the worst kind of lowlifes. It was a city job, and maybe the only requirement was that you had to have spent time behind bars at Riker's Island.

As the train made its way from the Upper West Side to the track, he recognized the sorry faces of the regulars when they boarded along the train route. They rarely acknowledged each other, somber faces buried in their favorite tip sheets and racing columns. Hunches, tips, and premonitions—whatever the bettors could conjure up, they kept secret. If you had a winner and they picked a loser it had nothing to do with anything other than dumb luck. It was as if their bad luck was an exercise in low-level schadenfreude. Matty lost the daily double and was down six bucks. The next race there was one gray horse entered. To Matty it was a clear signal, as it must have been to every other desperate bettor. No luck, he thought after the finish, adding to the torn-up tickets decorating the grandstand floor. "One more race and I'm outta here," he whispered to himself.

The early enthusiasm gone, it left him feeling cold, colder than his picks. He counted what was left of his original stake. Seven dollars and thirty-six cents, and that was the three-number combination he bet on. After all, no other hunches seemed to work for him.

When he cashed in the ticket it was for eight hundred dollars. To him, it was all the money in the world. He looked around, making sure that his lucky hit wouldn't make him a target. After all, he had made a friend of Phil by keeping him from being robbed after a big payoff. He sat himself upstairs in an area almost deserted during the winter. Splitting up the larger bills, he stuffed them into his shoes under his socks, making sure to double knot his shoelaces. Downstairs again, the rush of his extraordinary luck convinced him to stay until the end of the racing card. The sun streaming through the trackside doors warmed his favorite bench. He would get some coffee after his next bet. It might keep him from dozing off between races.

The conductor of the A train shook him awake. "Buddy, off you go. This is the end of the line. Inwood station. Where the hell are your shoes?"

Matty pulled himself up. He'd slept through his stop. On the ride back downtown, the cold train floor made its way up through his socks into his body. His shoes, and his winnings stuffed inside them, were now someone else's good luck. He got off at the 110th Street stop. By now, his feet were almost blue from the cold sidewalk. If he had been robbed of his socks and even his pants, it wouldn't have made a difference. By now Matty had damned himself to hell a million times over. He turned onto his street and there, in the omnipresent mountain of garbage bags and loose refuse, was a thrown-away pair of sneakers. Jamming his feet into them, Matty made his way up three flights of stairs to his apartment. Pockets turned inside out, he counted what he managed to salvage. The eight hours since his first losing wager seemed a century ago.

"Learned a lesson, jerk?" he repeated to himself. With the dimes and quarters added to the dollar bills, it came to almost his original stake. Hey, to a horse player, it could have been worse.

BORED OF EDUCATION
George Lantay

Deep psychological pathologies keep you from effectively functioning in the public schools (in any capacity). You cannot learn what we want to teach you. You won't read one word at a time. You won't sit quietly at your desk (with your hands folded). You won't say, "Yes sir!" or "Yes ma'am!" You don't march neatly in a row, not to assembly (in the morning) or recess at noon time or even after-school activities. You don't do your homework. You fail our achievement tests. You won't write ciphers (neatly in a row), add, subtract, divide, or multiply. You won't memorize the multiplication tables, the presidents of the United States, or state capitals. You can't draw maps of Europe or Asia or anywhere else. You don't know geography, geometry, algebra, trigonometry, or calculus. You don't know biology or chemistry or physics and you can't pass regents exams.

What good are you? What did you say? What does all this have to do with earning a living, your life? What do you mean, we never taught you first aid or childcare or how to get and hold a job? Of course we stopped teaching wood shop, metal shop, air conditioning and refrigeration courses, automotive repairs or cosmetology. We want you to learn word processing and how to sit in front of a computer screen and browse the Internet. We want you to watch Sesame Street and soap operas, so you learn to shop at the mall, spend all your money, buy new clothes, new cars, new houses and join the army, navy or marine corps, fly a plane, buy life insurance and die.

WHEN I FELL
Marilyn Solares, Age 12

Today in class I was mad at Maria and then when I had to go get my book bag I tripped over my book bag belt and fell and hurt myself really hard. I fell on my face and hurt with a metal on the side then I went to the nurse after that I called my mom and I told her to not pick me up. Then during math I had a headache then we went home and I did not see Jonathan.

YOU THINK YOU'RE HIDING
Barry Blitstein

You think you're hiding.
No.
I see you seeing me.
I see your fingers.
Teeth.

I hear your dog's heartbeat.

I won't move.
I'll quiet my breath,
Slow my heartbeat.

You'll wait until your dog dies.
You'll die waiting.

My forever is more forever than yours.

IF NOT NOW
Ark Stone

Be not caught up in Road Rage.
That is the way it is. Everyone
have to find their place in the sun.
The one find it sooner.
Another take a little longer.
Get up, stand up for your rights.
Do not give up the fight.
Heaven help us all. Heaven
help the one who turn their back away.
One who suffer one more day. Heaven help us all.
Get up, seize the time. One can make it.
People have to wake up to their higher self.
Some might say do not get too charged up.
What work for one may not work
for another. That is the way it is.
Take into account the planet
and world one find oneself into.
Sometime one cannot see from looking.
That is some trip for life for one to have.
Know that one in their fine state is there.
Then one will be in a better state.
Check it out for oneself.
Let no one turn you around.
Do not give up.
Rest if you must, but do not.
Just hang on in there at all cost.
People, people, people.
Let's get into getting. Seize the time.
People who need people are

the most blessed people in the world.
That is the way it is.
We have to open our heart and soul and make
the world a better place.
That is the real deal.
Be all that you can be. Give it what you got.
That is a lot to the one who is given much.
Welcome to the world.
Some say the eyes do not lie. Amen.
Smiling faces sometime do not tell the true.
Listen to what I tell you cause I have proof.
People, people have to get over
before they go under.
That is the way it is.
Happiness, love, peace.
Let there be joy in the world.
Start with oneself. Start with one self.
That is it. Start with oneself.
We are friends for life.
That is the way it is.
Inner voice.

RACE
Shirley N. Bland

I, Shirley N. Bland
I'm so sick of race
Always in my face, each and every day
From Monday to Sunday, from morning to night
Some days bright, some with no light
Of course this isn't no special time, any time will do

One day I'm going to make and
Take me some mace, some place and
See what happens to me
I, Shirley N. Bland, and the race in my face

TRUSTWORTHINESS
Zoe Eiffel

I thought I saw
Trustworthiness
How is one to know
What's what?
What's real?
What's true?
What's here to stay?

The world today
is so quick-paced
Movement is all that matters,
whatever forms a blur.
If it's not moving fast enough,
out with it.
It can't matter if you can fix
your focus on it.
If it's something you're sure
you saw, forget it.
If it's something you only thought
you saw, consider it.

That is the world we're living in.

UNTITLED
Gerry Bogacz

History shows
That you can't kill everyone
Who might do you harm
And there is no justice
In the attempt
It would be like
Executing everyone
Who might commit a crime
Before they do so
But we all have that potential
Pre-emption
Is just this side
Of genocide
It will not make us safer
It does not make us right
It is a blot
On our values
There are many dimensions
To justice
It's not for the simple-minded

LOVE LOST
Ark Stone

It is not about you.
Belittle another to make oneself big.
It is not about one having faith in another.
Have faith in oneself.
It's not about listening to another.
Listen to oneself.
Inner love is key. It is not about trust in another.
Trust in oneself when one is true headed.
Be one to pick up on it.
Be not one to say to another
that one is a liar, liar, one is on fire.
Let the truth be told by oneself.
Try telling a one that they look good
and whatever they are doing to keep it up.
Do not forget who your brother buddy friend is,
who is the one that is about positive.
Let no people place or thing come between that.
Keep inside of oneself
that he is there for your well being.

Please please please
do not have anything but a open heart mind soul.
One could be on earth a thousand years and
neva come close to the answers.
When one have a buddy brother a friend
and pick up on the fact they are a healer,
spreading harmony, let it be human,
excellent, against lies.
One can find oneself to be

a drummer and writer.
Take care take care take care,
say hi to another one.
Want that person to feel good.
Make oneself a light of happiness to the beings
one make contact with on the road of life.

Be happy be happy be happy.
Join no one in a petty party.
Let your light shine.
Let us the people not be blind
cause our eyes see only glitter
close to the things that set one free.
Somebody watches you.
One have to watch oneself. That is the self.
Check out oneself, check out one self.
Now is the time, be a upbeat person.
That is the way to check it out for oneself.
Now is the time. Seize the time.
Stand up. Then one will stand tall.

NO MORE
Kim Storms

I don't ever want to do this again.
Fall, bump my head,
get high.
There is a monster within me, that
scares the hell out of me.
It's ferocious and fierce
and knows no mercy.
But, I've learned, there is a way
to subdue that creature and the vile measures
it takes to bring me down.
I talk.
Plain and simple.
I talk.
I tell on it.
If others know of its sick behavior,
it can't hurt me.
I know it will always be a part of who I am
and the woman I have grown to be
but…
the exposure and the light
will protect me from it.
It can no longer afflict any pain, hurt, or anger.
Yes,
Today I live vibrant and new,
and…
my addiction no longer controls me,
nor do my behaviors.

PREJUDICE
Linda Thomas

You were born out of fear
As a seed you could be planted
in anyone, anywhere, at any time
Young children, middle age, teens,
and older adults
Blacks, whites, any person of color

You are so influential, or so you think
You say you decide if someone
        can move into a certain neighborhood
You say you make people cross the street
        to avoid others
You posted signs saying certain people
        were not welcome here
Couldn't join your "country's" club
Couldn't get an education here
Whether someone loves someone or not
You even took credit for that

You don't discriminate, prejudice
        You like to hate
Prejudice, it's time for you to
        dissipate

ONE GHOST TO ANOTHER
Theresa Keis

"Where are you going?"

"I'll be back," was the answer. The friendly ghost replied and left quickly.

"What have you been doing?"

It was getting dark and colder; the night settled for good.

"Well, I looked through the attic. It was that photograph of the couple on the beach I saw earlier. I miss them so much. I wish to see them again, and that's not until next season. Oh yes, I know what you mean, that I won't see them again. Why, why's that?"

"Well, they entered a regatta. Something terrible happened. It was, it was they both lost. It was too much for them. They just couldn't go on….they couldn't go on."

"Maybe they had it in them to become more like us."

RUDE AWAKENING
Suzanne Lapka

Break down
World askew
Mind injured
Dimples in forehead
Back broken
Eyes burning
Hand scarred
Walk floating
Off balance
Out dated
Dinosaur revived
Sex evaporated
Child absent
Nightmare, "daymare"
Pills powerful
Side effects blaring
Never dwell here
Gloss over ugly
Embrace the wonders
Hurray third year of new life

UNTITLED
Raquel Hill

When I want to die I sew instead. I began to put together all the bad and good times that I've had. Not knowing which is going to have more pieces. I wish the needle didn't go so far in. I wish the doctor didn't tell my mom to push. I wish I could just run out of material. How does it feel when it's the end? How does it feel – in and out – loop? Remember to fucking pull the string out [?] you made me stab myself. I give up because where life began for me is where it's going to end. Leave me in the womb, don't push me out. This scar will be here forever and pieces to this puzzle will always be missing.

VAMPIRE AND WEREWOLF
Precious Wilson

>have u ever seen ur twin
>not ur biological twin
>the other person who helps u
>make decisions

Have u ever made a bad decision? Well! Angel was going 2 school 1 day, when she ran into 2 school friends. Street & Play. They suggested we all cut school. At first Angel was reluctant.

Street said, we r never absent. 1 day won't hurt.

Play said, I'm havin problems in school. I'll never pass anyway.

Angel said, I'm on the honor roll. 1 day won't hurt.

So they cut school n went 2 Street's house. Angel's mom said, never 2 people's houses or cut school!! Angel didn't know Street and Play had other intentions. When Angel arrived they started drinking & havin fun. Playin video games, laughin.

Suddenly some guests arrived. Males & females. They continued havin fun. Ace asked Angel 2 dance. That's when someone slipped a mickey in her drink. 10 minutes later she felt ill, then suddenly passed out. Yes! unfortunately they took advantage of her.

2 AM. Mrs. Street walkin in. What!! is goin on here?

Mom, hi mom. Wait, it's not what u think!

Get these people out of my house. OK!

Mrs. Street, Angel said, can u please call my mom. I feel sick.

Mrs. Myers, Angel's mom, took her daughter home. A month later Angel is pregnant. Of course the family is very upset. She too young. She explains 2 her mom, she passed out and was taken advantage of by Street.

Mrs. Myers and Mrs. Street decide she should let the court rule. They stayed together. The baby boy was born.

But Street 4got 2 tell her something. He had been bitten by a Vampire 3 weeks ago. She stormed 2 the bathroom. Confused. Lookin at her neck, there were 2 incisions there.

But *she* has a secret!!! Angel was bitten 2 weeks ago by a Werewolf.

A month passed. Suddenly they transform to a beasty. Bump heads n battle 2 the end.

2 be continued.

DIAMOND
Carmen Coception

When my dog died, I felt very sad and lonely, because she was my life.
I had to put vegetables, carrots, potatoes on the table for her.
If I didn't do it, she would get mad at me.
She used to sleep with me.
But soon I'm going to be happy,
because my friend is going to give me a puppy from her dog.
So then I can be happy.
But I think it's not going to be the same.
She used to play with Ruby the cat and Queen the bird.
I'm very sad. I'm going to miss her.

UNTITLED
Jenny Lynn Adames

This heart pumps fast
the blood goes thru
my body cut open flesh
a lot of heartache a lot of pain
My flesh can't be changed
black and blues that are no one's
heart can't ever change Fuck it
this pain will never go away
this wall I built so high
and beautiful No cracks No flaws
you can't get in and I can't get
out this broken heart is made out
of steal and now its pain can never
be fixed

I AM FROM
Najaya Royal, age 10

I am from your mind
Your lost thoughts you left behind
I can see you try to be me
but it's just not good enough
I know you think I am old
So now you sold your love
for popularity and you know
what you get back is nothing

THE TIGHTROPE
Muriel Gray

The tightrope dancer was the prettiest member of the traveling circus. Golden curls covered in silver glitter twirled about her head as she performed without a net. Her elegant long limbs and pointed toes were a marvel to the earthbound audience as they gazed up at her. Dancing high over the sawdust, near the top of the tent at county fairs, she seemed an angel of light and grace. Dressed in a pink tutu trimmed in silver spangles, her tights and slippers were a perfect match. Above this magical effect, she held a fringed silver umbrella to give balance to her fanciful moves.

One fateful day, the umbrella flew out of her hand as she executed a difficult turn. Miraculously, she continued without a misstep. The umbrella was not so fortunate. It lay mangled on the floor of the tent, a harbinger of what could happen to her beauty should she have collapsed as well. A clown with a broom swept away the broken pieces as though part of the act.

We all walk the tightrope every day. A precarious future lies in wait for those no longer able to stay on their toes.

TO MY FAVORITE LUCY
Raquel Hill

                I don't won't to worry anymore I don't want to be scared
        Fair can last for a long time but I don't think I can bare it
    Being lost in the world it's hard mostly because I don't have a place to score
I try to ignore the struggle and pain but I always seem to get more
    Being poor isn't the problem it's enjoying life when you have so many options
Be good, be optimistic and remember most of the best had to deal with it too

HERE IS WHERE I ESCAPE

HERE IS WHERE I ESCAPE...
By Shaquanna Cole

Here is where I escape
Alone from the crazy world
Around me
I found inner-peace and joy
It is all because there is no noise
I take out my diary
And write all my history
Beginning from the past
And all the things it has taken
Away from me
To where I am now in the present
Where happiness befriends
Me
When I write I am peace
I can set my soul free
With each stroke of
My pen
I let everything out that I
Had within.
Writing is better than any medication
Or drug.
Especially when it comes from
Your soul and all the things
That causes
Pain.

I PRAY YOU, OUR ARTIST
Dev Rogers

I pray you, our artist,
Your creativity will yield a wonder.
Give us an exquisite picture
To grace a mellifluous presence
It will be a shining for us all
Resilient to criticism
Disdaining the paradox of witless envy.

STRANGE FRUIT
Lorraine Beyer Theordor

Poets and painters can create masterpieces
of this plump, petite fruit.

I wonder at the unconscionable act of nature,
that of a hard pit, lurking in the body of
this luscious fruit, ready to pounce on the
unwary, as I can attest to, with my broken
tooth.

The cherry reminds me of the last drop of blood,
or the dot at the end of a perfect sentence.

PARADOX
Zoe Eiffel

the paradox is
that what is exquisite
isn't necessarily creativity
what is shining ugly
can be mellifluous
in its resilient depth
the work of a true artist

SONNET
Bob Rosen

Behold the confluence of brilliant thoughts
Though restless rest it impede
Seek the reasoning of love unbought
To speak of how we need
What fardels we might bear
To burn the corpse of wry disbelievers
Harken, harken, we will give ear
To the screams of over achievers
To study, study hard the tomes
Written in secret in dark places
In form and stanzas like ancient poems
Blank of eyes, pinched the faces
Do I judge who will not protest
Am I as silent as is the rest

WHERE DOES CREATIVITY COME FROM?
Theresa Keis

Where does creativity come from? Maybe it stems from your inner self, maybe it's deeper than that, its deeper meaning goes on to…. What if, before birth—something happened. The light shone upon its dimensions that grew and turned into a prism of a relationship with God first, and love, and finally like an acorn it grew and grew into a beautiful tree.

Hence, where does creativity come from?

Say, I wish I were a tree—don't you see? The roots are at its foundation. It goes deeper and deeper.

We create further on its foundations. Our personalities with the world.

MAGICIAN
Pat Jackson

abracadabra
        open says me
stroke the lamp
        —your reality
let loose the genie
        —creativity

Merlin,
        hocus pocus
magical genius
        take us
                on your flight
        give us
                super sight

People of wizardry
        de facto parallel
fabricate your fantasy
        cast your spell
                masquerade physicality

Visionary of the mystery
        setting the flare
for visionless to see
        to strip us bare
                to set us free
                        beyond…
                              reality

WHEN IT ALL BECOMES TRUE

WHEN IT ALL BECOMES TRUE
Lisa Fenger

It is something like being a movie director. You dream up a terrible scenario or someone hands it to you, and then you are off, letting your imagination run wild: was there a school next to the nuclear plant when it exploded, did the airplane crash into a mall crowded with holiday shoppers, is the strong wind circulating the poisonous gas, how many dead, how many injured, how many missing never to be found. It's exhilarating, running these worst case exercises, and exhausting too, always something you didn't do well enough, you failed to get food to that whole city block, forgot the elderly at the top floors of the apartment building with no way down, ran out of resources and time, did not play well with your fellow disaster volunteers, first responders, and recovery workers. But in the end, you are just playing, playing a deadly game, to be sure, but playing nevertheless: dreaming of the worst, practicing the impossible to predict, running through in an hour, an afternoon, a day, a disaster that in reality would unfold at a pace both terrifyingly rapid and somehow also time-stoppingly slow, at the speed of disbelief and of shock.

And then the instructors call stop, and you shake the hands of the strangers you worked with, strangers no more in the atmosphere of the life and death decisions you made. You walk unsteadily out of the building or out of the area where the drill was staged and blink at the houses still standing and the people unaware of what you just experienced, the most horrible things that could happen to you, to them, to any of us, all of us, and you shake your head to clear it of those haunting thoughts and plunge back into the world again.

These are the pictures in your mind as you write the plans for feeding and sheltering the people of Minneapolis, should the worst ever happen, a terrorist blows up Mall of America, the bridges collapse up and down the Mississippi slicing the city in half, there is a nuclear leak, an overturned chemical truck, a gas explosion, deadly biological substances released. You fill your thoughts with horrors and write: this is how we would serve the meals, this is who we would serve and when, this is where we get the food, this is who we have on staff, these are the precautions we'd take to avoid becoming victims ourselves, this is the place we'd provide for the dazed and scared people who no longer have a safe place to live, this is how we'd care for the young and old and those with special diets and needs, and those uncomfortable in a mixed gender settings, this is what we'd tell them about their pets, their loved ones, their homes and businesses, this is how we'd comfort and inform them, this is how we'd somehow get them back to a life as similar as we can make it to how they lived before the disaster.

You are sitting in the call center as you write these plans. A disaster has happened to the very place you sit, Hurricane Isabel just last week and you are working the overnight shift taking a few calls here and there, people with trees though their houses and not enough food, spoiled meat in the freezers from lack of electricity, and clothes beginning to mold from the rain leaking through the roof, people just wanting to have a voice to talk to in the dark. You know something of what they tell you: you drove through the storm yourself on the way to your volunteer work answering the phones, drove around downed tree limbs and debris from blown out signs, you stood in the dark and watched the transformers blow with frightening blue light as the city slowly went black in the wail of the wind over the roof and stinging pulverized rain. You were there in Virginia, just outside of Washington DC, taking care of the people hit by the hurricane, and when the calls stopped coming at two in the morning, you wrote, imagining disasters befalling your home in Minneapolis.

You had come to the world of disaster response by accident some might say, and others might say through the evil plans of fanatics to hijack planes and crash them into US landmarks, like the Pentagon, like the World Trade Center. They set these plans unbeknownst to you, and the small but desperate cry of help that summer from the FBI agents a few blocks from your office in downtown Minneapolis warning of the plot went unnoticed, and in the next few weeks the scheme unspooled, the hijackers bought airplane tickets and the same day you bought airplane tickets and you'd meet up in Manhattan, the ten of them dying a fiery death and bringing down thousands with them in the planes and collapsing towers and you'd watch hopelessly, helplessly and swore the next time you'd never be that powerless again. And as soon as your eyes lost a fraction of that traumatized stare, and you were home again in Minneapolis, you signed up to help other people newly traumatized from house fires, tornadoes and roof collapses. And it did you good to have someone to save, to comfort, to care for in the name of those you couldn't help that bright September day, and slowly your stare began to recede, and those you worked with made you a leader and you worked at it ferociously with the energy born of passion and pain.

And slowly the planning and practice paid off. The volunteers you lead became confident in their jobs, understood the routines, could lead on their own without looking to someone else, and by the time you decided to move to New York to live among the people of the city whose hearts broke and raced with fear in exactly the same way as your own because of the horrible hour you shared, you went knowing that you had made a safe spot in a heaven-forbid-it-ever-happens chaotic disaster, that those you trained were now so good that they put their leader to shame, and you were no longer needed.

And so you moved and within weeks found yourself standing at the mouth of the Mississippi, the other end of the river you knew every day for a decade, and you stood on the broken levees of drowned New Orleans, trying to see a way to ease the suffering as the residents came straggling back, using the last of their money on gas to get home to their ruined warped houses, and you never thought you'd ever stand again in a city smelling of death, and yet here you were, helping in the only way you could by looking into those haunted eyes of the people before you and saying nothing because there were no words for what Katrina and those who abandoned her victims had left behind. And you go back to New York, shaken by what hurricanes can do, and you take the warnings of planners seriously when they say New York could suffer the same, and you practice and practice the unimaginable, what if, what if, what if.

And then the day comes when what-if becomes it-is-happening, only it is on TV, far from New York, back in your city, your Minneapolis, a bridge has fallen down blocks from where it all began for you, when you decided to fight the fear of falling towers by helping those in need. And now they are the ones in need, the same people you planned to take care of, planning so thoroughly knowing it could never happen, a bridge across the Mississippi could never fall down but what if it did. And you are helpless again, helpless like you were at the mouth of the great river in the dried mud of the floods, helpless yet again stuck in New York until you remember the words you wrote in the aftermath of a storm named Isabel. Who do we feed and how do we do it, who do we shelter and how do we console. Who entertains the children while their parents agonize. How do we organize and how do we make sense of senseless unbelievable tragedy. And you comfort yourself in the only way you can, with faith that those words have endured and now are guiding the ones who give food and shelter to those fallen suddenly in their cars fifty feet into the river and somehow survived, and to those who wait for the dead to be pulled from the wreckage. And you think that maybe there are people who can make the world a better place, and maybe that will never be you, but maybe, just maybe, you can do your own part to make it a little less bad on the day the unthinkable happens.

IMAGINE
Veronika Antoniadis, Age 13

Imagine all the people
who live on this planet with us.
And all the dreams forgotten,
the nightmares still fresh in their minds.
All the children left behind,
the parents who worry where their
children have gone.
All the rich people who haven't a care,
the people who suffer
through day, night, weeks and years.
Why government hates innocence
and children who haven't a name.
Imagine all the people,
whose lives slip between their fingers
and death takes place at all.

REVERIE OF MY HAITI
Carole Deeb

In reverie I remember
the women of my Haiti
walking down the clay-colored
dirt road to marketplace

Balancing huge straw baskets on the crown
of their heads one arm up
holding their treasured basket
filled with yellow boxes of Chiclets,
blazing red material,
buttons of all kinds and colors, penny candy,
and any barterable object
The burst of color in the basket seems faded
compared to their billowing skirts of tropical
greens, reds, yellows
and blood orange reflecting the jungle
Birds with wingspans that made one believe the palms
had taken flight into the warm tropical wind
Crouching in the marketplace
baskets between their legs
awaiting someone to buy their wares
Achete ici monsieur-madam can be heard
continually flung at the people passing
Seven mouths to feed and no one buys
Pleas of *Achete ici monsieur* to
the shoes walking by
The ton ton macoutes slither along the walls
Killers, I spit out quietly as they continue
slithering

Gunshots are heard and I realize it is not the
snakes
It is our people – it is a coup
At last we will have our city back

I touch my side and feel it wet
My skirt of tropical colors seepingly
Become red

Running—my blood
Running—my friends—blood
mixing with the red clay road

I am dying—
One bullet will kill seven mouths

THE CREEK
Claude H. Oliver II

The grass grew tall around the creek. However, today the creek was different. There were many flies buzzing about. There seemed to be a larger number of crayfish and small fish about. As the breeze blew, a strange odor wafted over the creek. As she went toward the odor, her heart began to pound. The aroma was that of death. Her son had gone fishing a day earlier but had not come home. Normally, she would not have been concerned. Today, however, she remembered the stories of strange men who wore sheets over their heads to hide their faces from any connection to the awful deeds for which they were responsible.

She followed the scent to the shore of the creek. An ear-splitting scream from the bottom of her being issued forth, scattering the birds nearby, as she recognized her son's face, with an expression of fear and horror frozen on his face. His pants were stiff from the blood which dried in them. The flies had begun their age old ritual of helping flesh return to dust.

As she looked at her son, her mind traveled back to the pains of his birth. Part of her felt as if it had been killed, as she remembered suckling him as an infant, giving of her own substance to feed her growing child. She remembered that the child's father had to leave home during the dead of night to avoid meeting his own demise.

She bent down and cradled his head, the head of her pride and joy, her only child. She hugged his corpse to her breast one last time and then commenced to drag the dead child to the small cabin where she lived.

Once there, she went into the cabin to fetch her shovel, which was used for planting and snow removal. She began to dig a trench in which to plant her now dead son. That completed, she place him in the trench and covered him, placing a pile of stones over his head.

It was late in the evening when she finished the horrible chore. She went into the cabin and sat at the table. The full weight of all that had transpired pressed down on her and her body began to shudder, emitting deep mournful sobs as she faced life without her reason for being.

She woke up still seated at the table, her head on top of her folded arms.

It was a new day, but painfully empty.

DESTINATION: PROMISED LAND
Suzanne Lapka

Leban buried alive
Mommy with God
Village painful decimated
Yaacov takes my hand
Leave all
Pack little
Hidden Mommy's candlesticks
Choking back tears
Other side of the world
Go in Peace
"Send me your tired, your poor…"
A stranger takes my hand
Yaacov is deported
I implore, "Help me save my brother!"
Hideous liar America
Everyone lost
Yaacov vanishes on the sea
The streets are not paved in gold
But in tears
Ship to train to feet
Uncle Phillip is shamed
His charge is ragged and silent
A mansion appears
A maid emerges
Alone no comfort
Only English allowed
The maid speaks German
She schools me
Prepare to meet the people

America meets Lithuania
"We are not impressed."
A smile cracks my mouth
Polite. Quiet
I understand little
Watching intently
Sort out later
Yaacov save me!
Please God
I want to go home
Where are you God?

UNTITLED
Gerry Bogacz

I hate
The hate that lashed out
Of a clear blue sky
Into our faces
I hate
The hate with which
We've responded
To the blow
I hate
The differences
That were imposed
On me and others
I hate
The triggers that
Conspire
To lay me low
I hate
Being forever trapped
In this frigging
Waking dream
I hate
The body count
Of innocents
That only grows
I hate
This wretched
Stinking march
To a place unknown
I hate
The weaknesses
Within us . . .

I THOUGHT YOU SHOULD KNOW
Anne Samachson

I don't know whether anyone who wasn't here understands what life was like for us back then.

I've heard people from other places, even from other parts of this region, say things like "I know what happened, because I saw the whole thing on TV."

Me, I didn't see the whole thing on TV. Around that time, though, I did hear one report on a radio program. It was late at night, a couple of days afterwards. The host, who clearly was not in New York, said he was speaking to someone in Manhattan and asked his correspondent to describe the scene.

The cheerful, almost ebullient reply was, "Everything's normal here! What happened downtown really didn't affect most of the city – I'm right here in the middle of Times Square and the lights are on and the traffic is going and people are out riding their bikes and walking around and everything is fine. Really, everything is OK!"

And I listened, wondering where those people really were, whether they were anywhere near Manhattan, whether they'd ever been close to downtown, because I was in a New York that was most assuredly not fine. Where nothing was normal.

If you heard that program, or one like it, you probably think that everything occurred on that one Tuesday and the next day we all kind of picked up and moved on with life as usual. But of course, that didn't happen at all.

***

A memory from that morning:
Walking uptown, I saw a man in a dusty business suit near Union Square. He couldn't stop weeping and couldn't stop hitting himself.

He was walking, stumbling and beating himself up because he'd tried to help an injured woman he'd found lying on the sidewalk. He told me that he'd picked her up and carried her into 2 World Trade Center so that she would be safe.

"I'm so sorry" he said over and over. "I'm so sorry. I thought I was helping her. I'm so sorry. I'm so sorry. I'll never forgive myself."

***

That day bridges and tunnels were closed to traffic. So were the harbors, airports and train stations. The buses, ferries and subways were halted for most of the day and once they started running again, the trips that went through lower Manhattan were unpredictable.

I guess we all have our usual routes and routines that we follow, pretty much without thinking. Getting to work, visiting friends, going shopping — it isn't a daily crisis, where every day you have to walk outside, get in your car and say to yourself, OK, how on earth am I going to take the kids to school? How long will it take? Which streets will I be able to travel? Do I have the right

ID in case anyone stops me? Will anything terrible happen that will prevent me from getting there? If I do manage to arrive, will the school still be standing?

I mean, normal people don't think that way every time they have to go somewhere. They just jump in the car, or go to their bus stop, or get on their bike, and follow their normal routines. They know where they will turn, how far they'll have to walk, where they'll grab a newspaper and cup of coffee — the normal stuff everyone takes for granted.

And before everything happened, I did that, too. No brainwork required. After years of traversing the same route almost daily, I knew exactly how to get to the places that were important to me without having to pour over maps, consult with police or strategize with transit workers.

***

A memory:
Me, speaking to a cop at Times Square subway station: I'm trying to get an A train to Brooklyn, but they told me the A isn't running here. Where can I get an A train to Brooklyn?

Cop: Where are you trying to go?

Me: I'm trying to get to an A train to Brooklyn.

Cop: No, no, you can't think that way. Forget the train number, where do you want to go in Brooklyn? Tell me what part of Brooklyn you're trying to get to, and I'll try to help you find out if a train is going there.

Me: I want to get to High Street.

Cop: What's that near?

Me: The Brooklyn Bridge.

Cop: Forget it. What's another station for you?

Me: Can I get to the Jay Street station? That's not so far from where I live.

Cop gets on his radio, asks a few questions, and says to me: If you can walk over to Penn Station, there are trains running from there to Brooklyn. When you get over to Penn, just ask someone to put you on the train to Brooklyn.

Me, still not getting it: Will it be an A train?

Cop: Don't worry about the number on the train, the number doesn't mean anything. Just ask whether the train is going to stop at Jay Street. Good luck.

***

The television was useless. The phone was unreliable. Sometimes I had a dial tone, other times not. Sometimes I would hear it ring, grab the receiver and find that the frantic person on the other end was unable to hear my voice. "Are you there?" they'd ask. "Is anyone home? Hello, hello, hello?"

Unable to leave the area, my neighbors and I took to the streets where the rumors ran rampant: At a time when so many things that seemed unimaginable had happened, nothing was too outrageous to believe. We heard that the ATMs were running out of cash. The grocers were running out of food. The pharmacies were running out of medicine. The liquor stores were running out of booze.

We stepped out of our front doors into a landscape we didn't recognize. The bright blue sky was hidden by billowing gray plumes. Heaps of crumpled, singed papers blew along fences and collected in corners. Every street was filled with soldiers, policemen, National Guardsmen, all wearing helmets, clutching automatic weapons, standing shoulder to shoulder and peering at the horizon. There were Humvees parked by the playground in the spot usually reserved for the ice cream truck.

As evening fell we saw groups of schoolchildren walking solemnly through the streets, softly singing, clutching candles and flowers, ready to deposit them along the Promenade, within sight of the billowing clouds of smoke and dust.

***

A memory:
I stood inside the subway car, unsure of its destination but hoping to make my way home. I don't know what I said or did, or how I drew attention to myself, but somehow everyone on the train seemed to be looking at me and to know where I'd been.

As the car lurched through the darkness, an elderly man walked over and took my hand in his. With his other hand he stroked my arm, solemnly telling me that God had kept me alive for a purpose. He repeated the phrase over and over, telling me that I was supposed to be alive.

After a few minutes he was joined by an elderly woman who hugged me and said, "You're here for a reason. You are alive for a reason. You have to find out what it is."

***

Afterwards, the city was a different place. Certain areas were declared "hot zones" and were inaccessible to those who lacked the required ID (for example, if you lived on Gold Street, and you wanted to go home, you'd go to a checkpoint, show proof that you lived on Gold Street and you might be allowed access).

Buses, once they were again running on some sort of predictable schedule, switched their routes nearly every day. OK, yesterday the bus drove on Broadway; today the same bus will run on Church Street; tomorrow, who knows?

The subway was the same way. We never knew from day to day which stations would be open and which trains were running on which lines. The maps were useless, out of date the moment they came off the presses, and new maps were being issued almost daily.

***

A memory, from a few weeks later, when getting a new, daily subway map had become the routine:

Entering a subway station, looking for the latest map, and being told that they only had yesterday's maps.

"Those won't do you any good," said the attendant. "Just wait a little while; we'll be getting today's maps in soon."

***

Because of the unpredictability of public transportation, and the ever-changing maze of barriers and security checkpoints, people who had to travel through Lower Manhattan couldn't really plan to be anywhere at a specific hour.

When you were able to figure out which train would take you to your destination, you'd go to the station and wait. And wait. How long between trains? Five minutes? Thirty minutes? An hour? Who knows?

The delays were endless and unexplained. Sometimes the trains would sit in the station, without moving, for long stretches of time. Other times a train would come to a sudden halt in a tunnel, the lights would go out, the air would switch off, and you'd sit in the dark, in silence, gripped in fear, just waiting for something to happen. No announcements. No apologies. No official word.

When you finally got out of the train, what would you find above ground? The fires at the World Trade Center burned for months; I think they finally went out in January 2002, but it might have been later.

Would you emerge from the subway and get a mouth full of ash? Would you find the street barricaded? Would the lampposts be covered with homemade posters showing the faces of the dead and missing? (Was anyone else struck by the fact that all of the faces on those posters were smiling? They were such happy faces, the photos taken at birthday parties, weddings and vacations.)

Even the most familiar places and people were suddenly strange. Thick layers of dust and ash ("don't think about what's in it") covered everything. Favorite bookshops and bakeries were transformed into smoldering heaps of twisted metal. Streets that had spent decades in the shadows of the now-crumpled buildings were suddenly flooded with light.

Photo identification was required to get into the bank and the dentist's office. Perfectly reasonable, rational people filled their homes with bottled water, batteries, dehydrated food and antibiotics and tucked gas masks into their briefcases before they dared to go outside.

***

A memory:
Towards the end of September, I noticed that people in New York stopped automatically saying "Have a nice day," and began saying something more sincere and more significant: "Be safe."

***

So, the politicians and broadcasters and self-appointed spokesmen told you that New Yorkers were strong and resilient, that they'd get through this just fine. And in a way, I guess that became true, although it wasn't true when they said it.

It became true, I think, because the people who weren't strong and resilient, who couldn't get through it just fine, ceased to be New Yorkers.

They retreated to their childhood hometowns. ("I'm writing to let you know I'm back home in Minnesota now." "I returned because I realized how much I missed California!")

They set out to places where no one knew about their pasts and they had the freedom to invent new selves. ("We're moving to Florida and starting over." "Everything is so different here in Arizona, we're making a whole new life.")

Or they just hauled themselves out to the suburbs and discovered a way of living that involved shopping malls, minivans and lawnmowers. ("We have so much room here — we have a yard!" "We'll still go into the city a couple times a year to see Broadway shows.")

So, they took off for places that they perceived as safer and easier, and the rest of us became, by comparison, by default, tough and resilient. Some people call us survivors, but most of us just think of ourselves as members of a club that we never wanted to join.

***

A memory:

I was told to list the items I'd lost but had a very hard time remembering what was in my office. I couldn't even remember exactly what my office looked like. I struggled, tried, made a cursory list and then gave up.

And then suddenly — about a year later — it was as though I awoke from a long sleep. I saw each detail of every item on my desk, every picture, every pen — all with perfect clarity. I was afraid to think about it too much, because I thought the image would disappear just as suddenly as it came. But it didn't. Everything is still there.

In my mind's eye, I can look out the window and see the gigantic Colgate sign in Jersey City, the light dancing on the surface of the Hudson and the ships silently passing on the river. I can look down, past the roofs of the World Financial Center, below the trees, and watch people walking around the cove.

I can walk around the 64th floor, go into the pantry, pour a cup of coffee and enter my office. I can sit in the swivel chair, turn on the computer, poke through the drawers — just as though I was still there. The black and beige scarf still hangs in the closet, David's crayon drawing is still taped to the wall, the shopping bag holding my new black suede shoes still stands beside the credenza, exactly where I left it Monday night.

It all seemed so real, as though the buildings still stood. As though everyone was just out to lunch or in a meeting, and, in a moment, they'd all return. As though nothing had changed at all.

***

It might already be common knowledge. You might already know what it was like. Perhaps you have already heard stories just like these.

But, perhaps not. Perhaps nobody thought to tell you. So, just in case you weren't aware, I thought you should know.

THERE IS A MAN I KNOW
WHO LIKES TO PUT GLITTER
ON HIS CLOTHES

SUBMARINE
Justina Jordan

There is a song that I like to hear that is called
"We all live in a yellow submarine"
And I wonder what is in
that dark deep blue sea
besides fish
And I think that going on a submarine
would be an excellent experience

(There is a man I know who likes to put glitter on his clothes)

I love to hear violins playing
on a nice summer night
while me and my friend walk together
holding hands
under the deep blue sky
with the moon shining

MAGIC'S ADDRESS
Jediael S. Fraser, Age 8

Magic doesn't live on Pitkin Avenue
Neither does it live on a street that's brand new.
Not in a hotel, a motel, or even a zoo.

It doesn't live with me
So, by chance, does it live with you?
At the end of a rainbow, inside a cloud
Or maybe with a Magician inside this big 'word' crowd?

In Texas, Utah or Italy?
I don't think it lives anywhere.
It shouldn't. Magic is, and should be, free!

IF I WERE A KITE
Caitlyn Klenner, Age 7

If I were a kite,
I would have colors like red, purple,
green, yellow, orange and blue.
The shape I would have is a diamond.
I would have two sticks attaching me.
When I go up I would feel the wind catching me.
I could see the whole world.
I could even see my house and other kites.

SEVEN WONDERS
Peggy Liegel

The decision committee rules that:
#1 is a yellow canary
#2 is tree bark
#3 is hog tied oops that's a mistake
#4 is red + blue = purple
#5 is the 24 hour sky
#6 is girl wonder kayaking for the 1st time through beaver builders built and what they built and how oh my.
#7 is the singing voice and music and communication's babel understood.

The decision committee rules that the committee is large and world filled and wonders never cease, that wonders can be decided again and again. The question is large and should not be contained. Seven is still a good #. Old wonders disappear, gone but footprinted and foolproof. The word wonder is key. The definition needs to be revised, resuscitated. What is a wonderful question word for anyone to answer better and better should they wonder why.

RITA DOVE
Paul Francois, Age 11

I was five in a photograph fishing with my grandpa when suddenly I caught one. The fish felt heavy and it was trying to leave me in the water and I was trying to leave him out of the water. He finally won the tug of war and I got soaked. I looked for it under water and saw nothing. Then I saw him. Bigger than Big. The one and only, the big, the bad and the best whale underwater. We fought as two lions fighting for their territory. And somehow I thought for a second, someone was going to win. Then unexpectedly a harpoon gun shot the whale. My grandfather saved the day. And the big, bad and best whale of them all was defeated and eaten. Hmm Hmm!

CLOUD PINK CAKE
Leen Shumman, age 8

Dear cloud pink cake
as though I have never tasted you
but I know how to bake you
as the clouds blush in my face
as it's windy and you are pink and soft
and you look so good
as though it is for my mom.
I still want to drown you down my throat
I call a water drain
I really miss how you taste
I know you will be sad
you will go down the drain
I still will miss you
when you flush down the toilet
as though you say goodbye
and I say goodbye to you
and I will be with you
you will not move
because I can see your tears
and your mouth talking
don't eat me
Never mind I want to see your tears
flashing and blushing down
like a cloud pink cake.
Wait you are that.

THE PROMISE
Allan Yashin

Harry and I had known each other for over forty years. We met in college and kept up the friendship through changing careers, various girlfriends, and Harry's eventual marriage and move to a big old Victorian house out in the sticks. I suppose they call it that because of all the trees, or maybe because the houses are usually made from wood, not bricks, but I don't know.

Then about two years ago, Harry's wife, Elaine, came home and announced that she had outgrown him. He was 57; did that mean she felt 65? Well, I don't know that either, but she packs her bags and leaves town and nobody ever sees her or hears from her again. So now Harry's living alone in a big old *empty* house out in the sticks.

For the next year, we sat around Harry's living room listening to jazz and watching old black and white movies from the thirties and forties. Harry's Dad had worked for one of the studios back then. No, he wasn't a movie star—he was an accountant, worked on the budgets of the films. Harry had grown up watching old movies with his Dad. Whenever one of his father's favorites came on TV—the Fred Astaire & Ginger Roger films, or the *Thin Man* series, any film noir mystery, and especially, *Citizen Kane*—Harry's father would cancel whatever plans the family had, and his father and he would watch the film together.

Harry told me that when VCRs were invented and you could actually *own* those classics and watch them whenever you wanted, his Dad said, "Harry, my boy, forget the parting of the Red Sea, *this* is truly a miracle."

So, now that his wife Elaine was gone, I'd come over two or three times a week and watch those old movies with Harry. Our mutual love for the movies was the glue that had kept our friendship together all these years. But eventually we'd get to the real business at hand, getting drunk and listening to Harry feel sorry for himself. I told him, "You know, Harry, one day she'll realize what a big mistake she made walking out on you and then she'll come running back home."

"Al, take it from me, she's definitely not coming back. I know it. And that's just fine with me. I'm just depressed because I wasted fifteen years of my life on her."

Then one night at around eleven, Harry calls me and says, "Ya gotta come right over. I've got something important to tell you." So, what's a friend to do, other than to think to himself *this better be damn important* but to say, "Sure, Harry, don't worry. I'll drive right out."

So. It's one in the morning and I'm sitting in Harry's living room watching him pace the floor. He's wearing pajamas and an old bathrobe but his bloodshot eyes make it look like he hadn't been getting much sleep lately, and his five o'clock shadow had a five o'clock shadow.

"Al," he says, "Al, I can't take it out here anymore. Living in this damn big old house, a million miles from nowhere. I've had it here. I'm going to sell it and move back to the city."

"Harry, haven't I been telling you *just that* for the past year?"

"Yeah. Yeah, you were right, Alsie, but you gotta make these decisions for yourself, when it feels right. And I did it today. I'm signing the papers next week and I'll be outa here by next month. That's why you hadda come over. There's something I gotta show you! Come on down to the basement."

"The basement! I've been coming over to this house for over fifteen years and I've never been down in the basement. What's going on Harry?"

"Nah, I can't tell you. You gotta see for yourself."

And Harry walks into the hallway and motions for me to follow him. He opens this door that I'd always thought was a closet and he flips on a light switch. What looks to be a sixty watt bulb casts a dim light on a rickety old staircase. Harry starts to walk downstairs. "Come on, Al," he says, "Come on!"

I watch Harry walking down that staircase and then he trips on his bathrobe belt that's been dangling beside him and he makes a grab for the banister, but there *is* no banister and he rolls headfirst down half the flight. I gasped, but when I rush down the stairs to him, he's already getting up and brushing himself off.

"This damn house! See what I mean?"

I was really glad he wasn't hurt, but now that I was down in the basement, I couldn't help but look around. That tiny bulb didn't shed much light, but it didn't have to, because the basement was totally empty. "Harry," I said, "why'd you bring me down here? There's nothing here."

"Yeah, well, I removed the evidence."

"Evidence! What evidence? What do you mean *you removed it?*"

"Al, look, stop talking! I want you to promise me something. We've been best friends for forty years, I can trust you, *right?* I'm gonna show you something no one else knows about and you gotta promise not to tell anyone else. OK?"

And he takes me by the hand and drags me over to the big filthy boiler in the corner and he points to a small door hidden from view behind all the pipes. "It's in there!"

It's in there, I'm thinking. What's in there? And what evidence did he remove? And then it all falls into place. His wife Elaine—the way she just disappeared. No one ever seeing or hearing from her again. And Harry telling me he knows she *definitely* won't be coming back. And now he's dragging me over to some secret room and making me promise not to tell anyone what I see. Oh my God. It couldn't be that, could it? Not Elaine's body.

"Come on, Al," he says again. "It's in here."

I didn't want to go in there. I was too afraid of what I would see. But when Harry yelled, "Al! Would you get in here? And remember that promise," I swallowed hard and followed him into that little room hidden behind the boiler.

It was dark in there. The only light was from the small bulb in the other room. I squinted and tried to look into the dark corners of the room, even glanced quickly behind a big easy chair that was the only piece of furniture.

"What are you looking for, Al?" Harry asked.

"You know Harry. You know. Where is she? Where'd you hide her?"

"What are you talking about, Al? What's wrong with you? *Oh, I know.* You're talking about Elaine. You think I did something to her. Well, take a good look around. I don't think you're going to find any bodies down here."

Harry turned on a small light and sure enough—no Elaine.

"Harry, I feel like an idiot. I'm sorry. I guess we've watched too many old mysteries together. But what did you mean about hiding the evidence?"

"Al, I meant the evidence of living fifteen years with her. Anything that would remind me of all that wasted time."

"So then just what the hell are we down here for?"

"See for yourself, Al." And then I saw that the easy chair was facing a glass showcase that had been attached at eye-level to the paneled wall. Harry was standing next to the showcase and he motioned for me to come closer. A look of pride shown on his face. "Take a look at this, Al. Isn't it something!"

I walked closer to get a better look and just then Harry flipped a switch and the showcase was flooded with light. My mouth dropped open when I realized what I was looking at.

"Oh my God! Harry, that's not *real* is it?"

"Sure as hell is, Al. The original and authentic!"

And there it was. Bathed in light in that glass showcase, an object from film history as iconic as Dorothy's red slippers or the statue of the Maltese Falcon. It was Rosebud! The sled from Orson Welles' *Citizen Kane*. The answer to the mystery of the last word on the lips of the dying tycoon. The sled was charred from being put into a furnace in the last scene of the film, but the name *Rosebud* could still be clearly made out.

"Harry! What does this mean? Why is this incredible thing hidden away down in your basement?"

"Welles was in big trouble," Harry replied. "This was his first film, and the bigwigs at the studio were pressuring him because he was running over schedule. They were threatening to take the film away from him. Welles called my father into his office one day and told him, 'Bernstein, *we're* not going to let those philistines in the front office ruin *our movie,* are we?'"

"He called your father Bernstein? Wasn't that the name of one of the character in the movie?"

167

"My father said Welles called anyone Jewish Bernstein. It wasn't a slur. He just had too many high and mighty things on his mind to remember anyone's name."

"Well, what did he want your father to do?"

"He wanted him to lie to the studio about the amount of money Welles was spending on the film. He told my father, 'Bernstein, the choice lies with you. Let RKO know about the hundred thousand I've gone over budget, and they take the film away from us and turn it over to some *hack* to finish and it turns up on a double bill under some *western*. Or…you use that clever little mind of yours, move around a couple of decimal points, and let me complete this…well, I've heard it being called a masterpiece by some. What will it be, Bernstein? The history of modern film is in your hands!'"

"What an ego!"

"We're talking about Orson Welles here, Alsie."

"So what did your father do?"

"Welles was over six foot four and towered over my father by nearly a foot. When he comes up to your real close, belly to belly, and he puts that huge hand on your shoulder, looks you in the eye and talks to you in that voice that sounds like it's on loan from God? Well, you know what my father did!"

"And Rosebud? Rosebud was his payoff?"

"Welles called it a little token of appreciation from all the future fans of the film."

"What a story! But why the big secret? Why is it in your basement? Why isn't it over your fireplace or on loan to a museum? I mean, that's an incredibly valuable piece of film history. Your father could have sold it for a small fortune!"

"I know. Welles *did* get a fortune when he sold it."

"Wait a minute, I don't get it. If it's here in your basement, how could Welles have sold it?"

"That, my boy, is where the secret comes in. Welles full well understood the future value of that sled when he gave it to my father. That's why he made my father swear he would never tell anyone that he had it. Welles took a replica that they kept in the props department in case a replacement was needed. When he ran out of money about twenty years later, he sold it, and no one knew it wasn't the original."

"Nobody but *you and your father*. And your father never told anyone else, or tried to sell the original?"

"Look, I tried to convince him, but he would say, 'I made a pact with a genius, and I'm not going to betray it to make a few stinking dollars.' He kept it in a box in his closet at home. He lived in fear that someone would find out about it, or that his cleaning lady would discover it one day. When he was getting too old to take care of himself, he finally agreed to move in with me. And that's when I though of this room down here and realized we could finally get the sled out of that box and let my father get some real pleasure out of owning it.

'He would come down here, sit in that easy chair, and just stare at the sled for hour after hour. It was the true joy of has last few years."

"And now what, Harry?" I said.

"Now that he's gone and I'm moving out of the house, well, of course I'm going to take it with me. But you know, after all those years of my father keeping his promise, I guess I can't break that pact either. For my father's sake."

"And me?"

"Gee Al, I had to at least tell *someone* what I had. And who better to appreciate it than my best friend and lifelong movie buddy? But you remember that promise not to tell anybody anything."

"Don't worry, Harry. I swear: what happened tonight goes no farther than me."

"Good! Then you can help me dig up Elaine's body from the backyard. I gotta get it outa here before I move."

"Oh my God, Harry! Are you serious?"

"Maybe. What do *you* think?"

FUNNY DAY
Shunn Theingi, Age 11

I wake up early
I get dressed and
Walk to school
When I got there,
I was early
I figured I forgot
To do my homework
So I open my book
And go to the bathroom.
When I come slowly to where my things are,
I feel frightened
I hid myself in the corner and saw the pencil
going up and doing my homework!!!
I calm myself down
I stay in the corner for a while
And then later, I go to my things.
I finish my homework.

When I line up
I saw my teacher Ms. Lovely
And you won't believe it because
She was fine yesterday
And today, she is a witch!!!
She had a long sharp nose, pointy hat and a magic ball in her hand.

When I line up
I saw my friend Susan and
Do you want to know what it is???
I saw a tail and Susan was a big cat.

I feel scared
Also, everyone is either
Cat, dog, fox, elephant, or crocodile.
Oh! My My My!

You wouldn't
Want to guess it
I mean what I see
In my class.
My class was neat and
tidy because we
cleaned it yesterday.
But today, it is a mess.
Papers were glued on the wall
Chairs and everything.
Ahhh!

Do you know that
my teacher doesn't
have a husband
but in my class
there was an ugly
monster. It said
"Hi, my dear" to my
teacher. The voice is
high and scary.

The day went
wrong and funny

We don't do
Any work
Because Ms. Lovely, the witch

Is always kissing or holding
hands with the ugly monster
I don't do anything
I just sat there
Staring at everyone
Everyone is messing up
the whole room.
I wonder
If I am in a funny magical world.
I decided I will go to
the principal at lunchtime.

Lunchtime, I went to the
Principal just like I
Decided but you wouldn't
Believe it. The principal
is a bee. It put poison
On me but before
He did, I ran out of the school.

But, outside there are people, not animals.
It is really a magical world
Inside school.

I NEVER
Donald Williams

I've never tasted French Food
I never touch a rat
I never smell bad
I never never like to hear bad words
I never want to see bad things happen

SUCKED IN
Joseph Francois, Age 9

One day Jake was talking a stroll at the beach. He saw lots of things like a surfing contest, a magic show and a splendid snack bar. Almost everybody was active there. One thing wasn't right. There was no tide so he went to the edge of the water and stepped into it. Jake got sucked into the bottom of the ocean where he fell in a robotic whale.

He heard foot steps coming his way. Before he could have got up and run a tall man came in the door. Although the man was tall, he was fat. He picked up Jake and walked back through the door he came from. There was a staff of guards all over the place. They were building a cannon in the whale's fin.

Jake knew that these people would get a lot of credit for the work they were doing. Jake kicked the guard in the leg and ran to the cannon but another guard grabbed him and brought him to the boss. The boss said to feed him to the sharks. Jake was so scared and shaking that he shook himself free.

He ran out of the room with no interest in staying in there. "These people disgust me," Jake said. Then Jake started to wonder if this place didn't exist and if it was a dream.

He was going to deposit himself out of that place. He ran to the cannon and when one of the guards tried to grab him he would slide under them. The cannon shot him—a direct hit. It made a lot of sense. He made a promise not to step in the water again.

PAPER BAG
Caitlyn Klenner, Age 7

I will put some things in this bag:
Candy from trick or treating and party streamers.
Some Barbie clothing and a marker.
A crayon from the Crayola collection.
Some glue sticks
a sock and a Barbie.
What else will I put in this bag?
The end.

THE FOX IN THE BUSH
Jediael S. Fraser, Age 8

There was a time when I went deep into the woods
Of dark, scary skies
And nothing to shine on the dark but the silver moon
Following me
I suddenly heard a rustle in the bushes
Some leaves being crumbled
And something's stomach rumbled
Then the moon presented to me
A fox in the bush.

I ran through the woods
Away from the hungry fox
It hit down a tree
It was strong as an ox
Then I trapped it in a box
I was free!
The fox away from me!

THE MAN IS JUNGLE DOG
Jude

Not long ago I was invited to vacation in South America. This came from an old friend; even though our course in life hath taken different paths, we still remained close tight-knit buddies. This fellow was a fortune hunter of sorts and was always seeking out new and uncharted territories for his adventures. I call him Jungle Dog.

One day while he and I were out in the field on the back mountains for a spell, we started trekking through the Colombian rainforest and other trail rated terrain. Throughout the journey however I kept sensing that something was not quite right. As my instincts would have it, I was right on point. Several secret Colombian police soldiers had been following us now for quite some time. Now we were completely in arms way, surrounded in an ambush, machine guns pointed at our heads as if to shoot to kill upon orders.

Out from behind one of them stepped the head cheese, one of the most brutal nefarious and merciless generals the Third World hath ever seen. His name was Octumia.

Unknown to me Jungle Dog had in his possession an ancient treasure map from an old Inca goldmine which was located somewhere deep within the Colombian jungles. The secret police had been onto him for weeks now. The general demanded he hand over the map. But Jungle Dog stood his ground. He was not going to part so easily with his meal ticket to what could probably turn out to be the ultimate jackpot.

Before I knew it, Jungle Dog broke loose and battled through the jungle thicket. I quickly followed suit and jetted like a Volkswagen. Machine guns began blazing everywhere and the army of soldiers was gaining ground very fast. As I unsheathed my machete and started cutting and slashing through the thicket, JD was just steps ahead of me. However, without warning the trail had come to an abrupt end, with Jungle Dog hanging for dear life over a cleft of the rocks.

We were several hundred feet into the air overlooking a couple of rocky high stony waterfalls. The secret army force was still in hot pursuit and was almost upon us as machine guns continued to blaze. Our options were fading fast. I had to start thinking really quick while we geared up for some accurate and precise maneuvers. I yelled for JD to, "Grab onto my hand, and I will pull up using sheer body twists to get you from the cleft."

As I caught him I pulled him back over to me with one swing.

"Now grab ahold and let's get a piggyback going," I said.

And I quickly grabbed for several vine thickets that were overhanging. With my trusty machete I cut and slashed their entanglement and within seconds we were doing a Tarzan swing with one move.

In one fell swoop, still hundreds of feet in the air, we became airborne and made an incredible landing onto the other side. Here came the Colombian secret police/army. No chance! Jungle Dog and I were safely on the other side as they came to a dead end, while we tried to take in the enormity and inconceivable feat that was accomplished. We calmly looked at each other, in amazement; and suddenly burst out with gut wrenching laughter.

We eluded the secret police army this time, but our adventure continues! That is a story for another day!

AN ODE TO SNOW
Osose Ebesunun, Age 9

Why don't you come every day?
Soft and clean while falling from the sky
When you go away I can't stop thinking about you
It worse than a test when you stop falling from above
Why are you so fun to me and my friends?

GOLDFISH
Marie Livingston

Looking at you in a tank of clear cool water
floating in a time zone spirit
not eating very much, you are very
colorful, with piercing eyes not blinking
I'm only your Keeper, the joy that I keep
watching you splish splash like a seal
in water

THE BIG BLUE BOX
Victor Sanchez, Age 10

I was walking in my house when I heard a knock on my door. I opened it and found a box. It said, "To Victor." I opened it and found a scarf. I was about to wear it when it attached to my arm. I stared at it; it opened up and inside it threw out instructions. I read it and it said I can turn into 11 creatures and anyone I stare at. I clicked it and turned into a big monster. I jumped around in my skin. I suddenly turned into a computer. Then I knew I get to turn into any metal thing. Then I clicked it again and it said "STILL NOT MADE." It made me turn into a human again. At lunch, I looked at my mother and clicked the thing. I turned into my mother. That's when something hit me. I get to turn into anyone I look at.

THE ADVENTURE
Vincent Sanchez, Age 12

One day there was a kid named Timmy. For Christmas what he wanted most was a mechanic robot. Christmas came around and he opened his presents very fast. He saw a teddy bear with batteries. He said oddly, "I don't want a teddy." He opened the window and threw the teddy out the window. The teddy landed in a trash can. He felt something lift up. He was in it. The trash man threw him into the trash truck and then he went off. He was thrown into an ocean and floated away. Ten days later he reached an uninhabited island with trees. He was different than other bears because he can walk, talk, and see things. He went deep into the forest and reached another bear called David and David's brother Jeremy.

To be continued…

MY THIRD EYE
Hayat Dhobhany, Age 9

My third eye sees
people
sneaking and stealing

putting it in your
pocket
My third eye is a
camera
seeing people using
the bathroom
EWW!
my third eye sees
different than my
2 eyes

TELEPHONE POEM
Qiiyana Simpkins, Age 17

You'll know the area code is 718
But the rest of my number you'll have to guess
The best part is it's in a joke.
Why was 6 afraid of 7?
Because 7,8,9.
Then there's a number with no real value.
And there's the number 7 ate.
Then the number with no value again
Then the number that fears 7.

WAITING
Syd Lazarus

Not all of us are sick in this large waiting room. Some are here for check-ups, shots, and other mundane things. Some very sick are waiting for an emergency room doctor—our partners and owner parents filling out the necessary paperwork. It's amazing how we all get along in this room—dogs, cats, birds, a squirrel and pot-bellied pig—waiting patiently, being admired and petted by the humans waiting. A K-9 dog with his policeman partner, a beautiful golden guide dog. It's very quiet considering how busy it is—no barks, meows, or squawks. Most sensitive to those of us who are truly ill. Doctors rushing around and announcements over a loud speaker—just like any big city hospital. Please don't cry, I say to my human. The doctors are good here. They call out our name.

GREEN
Isaiah Sanchez, Age 9

Green eyes, green head,
Green body lying dead,
Green book with a hook,
Green cook making gook,
Green Gatto with a patto,
Green potty with a body,
Green fish with a dish,
Green, Green, Green

MY ODE TO FALL (OH APPLE PIE)
Tanzania Coleman, Age 9

Oh apple pie why are you so yummy?
Every time I smell you being made
I smell hot cooked apples. The
yummy crusted nice hot delicious
and not burnt. The stuff between
the apple looks like yellowish
slime between some lime. Going into
my tummy it's so sad you're
so yummy!

BUTTERFLIES ARE COOL
Myint Myat Thinn Kyi, Age 8

Butterflies are colorful
Butterfly, butterfly you are
High up in the sky going through
Flowers and flowing through the Earth.
Asian American butterfly, butterfly.
I like because you are so cool and pretty
So colorful that I like you.
Butterfly, butterfly fly through the air dancing
All around go through the rainbow and now
You are near me and I am happy.

AUTOBIOGRAPHY OF THE COLOR RED
Karla Conford

I don't like the idea of someone writing about me. In the past, I found their research faulty. And the interviews, they are the worst. These people—biographers, researchers, journalists—have no imagination. I'd rather talk to a five year-old. In fact, I love talking to five year-olds. They have imagination and it has not yet been lost. And they are playful, like me. One of my specialties is changing tones. I go from bright red to deep red, orange red to blue red, pale to bright. And with each change of tone, a new term or description is invented. I do find it hilarious. And now that I think of it, the matter of associations comes to the fore. I recall those psychologists, psychiatrists, physicians all wanting interviews with me. Also, of course, the sociologists, anthropologists, artists and art curators alike, knocking on my door, trying to learn my secrets. My favorite visitor was the old farmer. I invited him inside and we had tea. He stayed for months instead of the usual hour, and we each learned so much about farming, planting, foods, nutrition. And then he died. Oh well—it's part of the life cycle! Oh yes, nutritionists, how could I forget. They love bright bright red, especially bright red tomatoes. They say it has more something or other—yes, I know it is lycopeneeeeee. I'm not a dim wit.

But I really loved it when the priests, rabbis, and imams came all together, to admire me and assign virtues to my various tones. I put on a wonderful display to make them happy. These people, meaning well, actually thought they found the secret to eternal life by watching me change my tones—ha. I didn't want to disappoint them, so I kept quiet and just changed colors. Finally, they left. I left as well and went to visit my friends in the garden. The robin red breast, the butterflies, grasshoppers, dragonflies, and my favorites, those cute lady bugs. They like the color red, too, and are amongst my special favorites.

FORTUNE COOKIE
Andrew Leong, Age 8

Once I went to a store.
I ordered a fortune cookie.
It took one hour and then it was here.
When I looked at it,
It was dancing on the plate.

HER NAME WAS LUCKY
Allen Raymon

I'm into dogs. Although it has been years since I lived with one.

She had her own chair, soft and comfortable. The chair was placed against the window. Since this was the ground floor she was able to put her front paws on the window sill. She carefully inspected each person who passed in her sight. If she decided they were not properly dressed, she would bark. She wasn't bothered by drunkards as long as they kept moving.

She hated rain, having to take a bath, or go near a pool. Anywhere, even a puddle.

Someone had the bright idea to teach her to attack. She just jumped on the wall.

Oh yes, she loved having her whiskers combed.

Lucky was a standard size Schnauzer. Most people were used to seeing the miniature. She loved obeying, such as at the Friday night card game, "Where do you go when we play cards?" She didn't hesitate—right to her chair, facing in the direction of the game.

When there was a select meal cooking for her, she wouldn't touch her dog food.

I was taking accordion lessons, practicing at home. When I hit a particular note, she would throw her head up and howl.

Don't know where I got the rabbit, but he had a place in the kitchen. Very alert each time the refrigerator door opened. Lucky was not happy sharing. We all went up for a country weekend. Lucky chased the rabbit under the house, never to be seen again.

MY ONLY FRIENDS
Isaiah Sanchez, Age 9

My friend is a mitten and my other is a baseball. They don't get along very well. So one lives in a cage and the other lives in the other cage. Every day I play with them. When I throw the ball it comes right back. If it goes over the backyard gate it comes back. I care for them a lot. One day the ball told me a secret. The secret was I got a hole. I got scared. I got a ball sewing machine and sewed it up.

THE NOSE NEVER LIES
By Joseph Francois, Age 9

This rock comes from the beach.
Everybody, it can't fool me
because the nose never lies.

MY MORNING RIDE
Allen Hoage

This morning I was on the bus and said to the bus driver, "Happy Valentine's Day." He said not a word, so I walked to a seat, sat down. I looked at him and said, "I hope you don't forget to buy your wife some beautiful flowers." Also on the bus were a lot of ladies riding and I said to them, "Happy Valentine's Day," and they said it back to me.

Valentine's Day is not only for ladies, it's for men too. Men get flowers also. When you see people outside say, "Happy Valentine's Day," and watch everyone smile.

WHEELS ON THE BUS
Myint Myat Thinn Kyi, Age 8

The wheels on the bus
dance all the way to school.
all the children were reading
at the blue school with frosty windows.
and the school turned red
when the pencils ran away.
the little yellow school bus
started to dance in the classroom.
and the children saw him and they
began to dance too.
The teacher came in and saw them
dancing so the teacher shouted to them
and the children said it's fun
so a snack began to come out of her dress
and the children began to laugh and
even the little yellow bus ran away.
The teacher said not to run away
so the little yellow bus stopped and said
"You are not angry with me?"
"Of course I am not angry at you!"
"Let's dance," said the little yellow bus
so they began to dance.

THE MOON
Andrew Leong, Age 8

The moon is so bright
I can see the stars at night
There are 9 faces of the moon
I like 2 moons
They are the full moon and the new moon
I heard that if you look at the moon
You turn into a monster

WHITE NIGHTGOWNS
Muriel Gray

The purity of white nightgowns
Suitable for ladies from birth to the grave.
Tiny and lace-trimmed for newborns
Growing larger with succeeding years,
Complimenting the teenager's changing status.
Perfect for the bridal night
Milk stained for a new mother.
Utilitarian as a shroud
Resurrected in clouds for harp-strumming angels.

EARRING
Mikhal Morris, Age 11

I am an earring.
I decorate my owner's ear.
I'm sometimes sparkly,
I'm sometimes dull.
I can be dangly,
I can be still.
I can be real,
I can be fake.
I am an earring.

THE YEAR I TURNED 10
By Joseph Francois, Age 9

The year I turned ten. No that's a lame title. How about the year I turned ten? Yeah that's right, that's a good title. "Hey you! over here under the stove." You said that title was lame. Liar. I did not say that you mouse. Yes you did. No I didn't. Wait a minute. I'm going crazy. Tell me about it. Hey, no one asked you to agree with me. Well you said that title twice, that's dumb. Shush, you little brat. I'm supposed to smack you up side your head with a broom. M, m, m, m. Hey don't give me that doggy face look, O.K.? I won't hit you up side your head with a broom. Great, now I can eat you. BOYS! Let's eat him. HELP ME!

MIRROR, MIRROR ON THE WALL
Syd Lazarus

How shall I begin? Once upon a time seems like a good start. My name is Snow White and I used to live with seven guys. Now I live, married of course, with a handsome prince. Back then it was another story, but a familiar one: beautiful girl, wicked stepmother or witch, spells, poison apples, you get the idea. All based on the jealousy of an older woman. Cinderella, Sleeping Beauty, Rapunzel, and I all had the same problem, though I felt bad for Cinder. She had a wicked stepmother and sister to contend with. We all wanted the same thing though, a happy ending. But to get back to my seven guys, they took me in when no one else would. I don't remember their last names—they weren't the same family—but their first names were Sleepy, Sneezy, Dopey, Doc, Happy, Bashful, and Grumpy. They were happy little guys, always whistling. That was their motto, "Whistle while you work," and they all had jobs. I took care of their house when they were gone all day. All of them were short—they were dwarfs. Today they would be called little people. It didn't seem to bother them. They were all happy and wanted to protect me. Once my prince saved me and we married I moved into his castle. We tried to locate my seven guys but they were gone. They had relocated and we couldn't find them. We wanted to thank them. I hope they are still together. I speak to Sleeping Beauty, and Cinder and I have become friends. We shop together a lot. She's got this thing for shoes. Life is good and I'm glad to tell you that everyone lived happily ever after.